The Enthusiast

Also by Peter Hill

The Liars

The Enthusiast

Peter Hill

Houghton Mifflin Company Boston 1979

First American Edition 1979

Copyright © 1978 by Peter Hill

Library of Congress Cataloging in Publication Data

Hill, Peter
  The enthusiast.

  I. Title.
PZ4.H64852En 1979 [PR6058.I4465] 823'.9'14 78-12039
ISBN 0-395-27543-1
Printed in the United States of America

S 10 9 8 7 6 5 4 3 2 1

The
Enthusiast

CHAPTER ONE

The sky above the mountains was cold-blue, streaked with high white cloud that hurried across the heavens as if pursued. It was early September and the clear sun gave a false promise of warmth to the coarse, stunted grasses and the primitive mosses and lichens which clung tenaciously to the upper slopes of Moel Celyn. There was an indeterminate line beyond which nothing grew, leaving the bald pate of the mountain exposed to the weak sun and the eager wind.

On an almost sheer rock face some way below the peak a yellow-clad figure inched along a meagre ledge leading to a narrow chimney, a cleft in the rock little wider than the climber's own body which, once scaled, would gain him another thirty feet or so. He moved slowly, which was indicative of both tiredness and experience. He had been climbing for three hours and he determined to rest before tackling the chimney.

He had left his lodgings in the town of Bala shortly after dawn and driven along the road that bordered the lake called Llyn Celyn, turning off on to a track and finally abandoning his car within what was for him an easy walk to the lower slopes of the mountain of his choice.

The climb he proposed for that day was no more than a training jaunt, posing no real problems, but offering a sufficiently severe test to hone his mind and body in preparation for the sterner climb to come. In a couple of days he planned to move on to Llanberis and from there tackle the climb to the top of Mount Snowdon. Moel Celyn was ideal for his purpose that day, there was the traverse across the face, the chimney, the steep bank of loose shale, then finally the fast climb to the summit. If he stood up well to that modest climb he could look forward to the highlight of his holiday with every confidence.

Now he wedged himself between two jutting rocks on the traverse and relaxed, breathing deeply of the air that had the taste of chilled wine and savouring the continual beauty of the mountain landscape. John Williams was a man content. What other sport or hobby was there to compare with his? He would return to the world refreshed in mind and body, the better by far for his lonely and mildly dangerous contest with the mountains he loved. He felt at one with the harsh beauty that surrounded him and was exhilarated by an almost spiritual sense of belonging.

Only those who had never done so could ask why men climbed mountains and then be surprised when they received an enigmatic reply. With some reluctance he eased himself to his feet and faced into the jagged rock, resuming the physical expression of his pleasure.

He thought he was alone on the mountain.

The killer was on the upper slopes before John Williams arrived. He watched as the climber made nothing of the lower approaches and selected the most difficult ascent to the summit. He approved of John Williams, approved of his evident professional approach to the climb. Williams was sensibly dressed, sensibly equipped and was evidently tackling a climb which was well within his capabilities. In particular the killer approved of the route Williams had selected, which would lodge him in the chimney where his progress would be slow, and of the bright yellow weatherproof jacket he wore which would show up well against the dark grey background of the rock. As a target, John Williams was ideal.

Once he was absolutely certain of the route Williams had chosen, the killer set about selecting his firing position. He knew

2

he had ample time before Williams reached the chimney and he chose his spot with care. He selected a thick spur of rock that jutted out at right-angles to the bulk of the mountain like a stiffened thumb and settled himself into a shallow moss-covered dip at the extreme end of the spur. From here, because the rock face was angled towards him, he would have an almost straight shot once the climber entered the chimney and he would be able to see the splash of a miss.

The climb to the firing position had not tired him but the physical effort had quickened his breathing and set his pulse racing. He placed the long executive-style carrying case down on the ground, eased himself down beside it and relaxed completely, knowing that Williams would take at least another half-hour to reach the chimney exit.

He allowed himself ten minutes' rest, consciously relaxing his muscles and controlling his breathing, then rolled on to his face and eased himself forward to look out over the rim of his hiding place. Williams was about to begin the traverse across the rock face, his bright yellow jacket standing out in sharp relief against the almost black rock.

The killer grunted his satisfaction and took his attention from his intended target to concentrate upon the conditions under which his shot would have to be made. He considered the direction and strength of the wind, the atmospheric pressure, the condition of light, the air temperature, the angle of fire and the distance to target. He drew upon his considerable experience and his natural talent in deciding most of the factors, but for the last, the distance to target, he sought the assistance of an Ordnance Survey map by use of which he calculated that he would be shooting over a distance of some 800 yards, give or take ten yards.

His inability to gauge the exact range concerned him a little, as did the uncertain air movements up here in the mountains, and he decided to allow himself three shots. He had put in a considerable amount of practice but this was, after all, his first recent attempt at a live target. There was no doubt that, even allowing for reloading and resighting, he could get off all three shots inside six seconds. He was that good.

3

This decision made, he returned the Ordnance Survey map to the thigh pocket of his camouflage jacket and rolled over to the carrying case, taking care not to expose himself to view above the rim of the hollow. The case had been black and of extremely smart appearance but he had camouflaged it, painting it in beige, dull green and brown in wavy lines. He opened it to reveal the rifle nesting amongst the foam rubber, and beside it the X6 telescopic sight, especially selected for its wide angle of view. From one of the voluminous pockets of his camouflage jacket he took a strip of dull coloured, patterned curtain cloth and laid it on the ground near the lip of the hollow. His precious rifle would not feel the cold damp touch of the wet ground.

The killer took his rifle from the carrying case and placed it carefully upon the strip of curtain cloth, the telescopic sight beside it, then looked over the rim of the hollow to check on the movements of his target. Williams had almost crossed the traverse, was nearing the chimney. Still the killer's movements were unhurried. He took great care in securing the telescopic sight to the rifle. He was a professional, a craftsman.

He assumed the prone position, body at an angle, legs spread for comfort and balance. He picked up the rifle and wound the padded sling tight around his left arm to minimize the recoil movement, cuddled the stock hard into his shoulder and looked through the sight. Williams was at the foot of the chimney, obviously resting. There was still ample time.

The killer relaxed his position and spent several minutes adjusting the focus and elevation of the telescopic sight, now and then taking a look at Williams to see that he had not moved. When he was absolutely satisfied he took three rounds of ammunition from his lefthand breast pocket, inspected them, polished them with a small piece of clean rag, then loaded them into the rifle.

When he took up his position again Williams was standing, about to begin the climb up the chimney. The killer eased himself up on to his elbows, ensuring that the barrel of the rifle was held clear of the rim of the hollow, and took aim.

Williams was moving slowly, feeling his way, crawling up the

4

face of the mountain like a yellow spider. The killer let him climb for a full minute, then prepared to shoot. His body relaxed at the order of his mind, his right eye nestled into the pad of the sight, his finger curled round the trigger and took up the first pressure. He exhaled gently but steadily, leaving his body absolutely still as he squeezed on the trigger, deliberately not anticipating the instant of firing.

The instant he had fired the killer worked the bolt action and reloaded, then resighted on the target. So fast was he that he was able to focus back on Williams in time to see the splash of the bullet as it struck the rock, level with the head of his human target and some three feet to the right. It was as near as he had dared to put his aiming shot without risking wounding his target and losing him before he could make the kill. So long as the climber did not fall from the chimney in sheer fright, that would not now happen. He would be stunned into inactivity, would not even hear the sound of the first shot before the second arrived.

The killer, knowing his first shot was high and right, aimed off to compensate, resighted and fired, just three and a half seconds from the moment he had first pulled the trigger. This time he aimed to kill.

He reloaded and resighted in time to see the bullet splash into the rock bare inches from the climber's chest, but to the left. Now he needed his speed to ensure the kill. The climber would have heard the sound of the first shot. There are two bangs, one from the muzzle as the bullet leaves the barrel, the other, the only noise Williams would in fact have heard, the whipcrack sound of the bullet breaking the sound barrier on its way to the target. Williams knew now that he was being fired upon and sheer terror might dislodge him from his precarious grip on the rock face.

The killer fired his third shot fractionally less than six seconds after the first. This time there was no splash of bullet on rock. Williams fell away from the rock face in a slow graceful plunge until he struck a projecting boulder 400 feet down the mountain and his broken body began a jerky, bouncing descent, a diminishing yellow dot tumbling in haphazard fashion until it came to untidy rest on the lower slopes of Moel Celyn.

The killer carefully packed the rifle and the scopesight back into the camouflaged despatch box. He was not particularly pleased with his performance. He could rightly tell himself that this shoot had been his first for a long time under field conditions. But he set himself high standards. He had taken all three of the shots he had allowed himself and he felt that he ought to have succeeded with two. Conditions had not been that bad, there was really no excuse.

Evidently he needed more practice.

When John Williams did not appear at his lodgings in Bala for the evening meal little was thought of it. The landlady simply assumed that he had decided to eat out and would return in his own good time, but when he did not appear for breakfast the following morning and she discovered that he had not slept in his bed the previous night, that his car was not parked outside the house and that none of her other guests had seen Williams since he set out to climb Moel Celyn the previous day, she telephoned the police.

In mid-morning local officers, reinforced by two men from the mountain rescue post at Blaenau Ffestiniog, discovered Williams' car and, a little later, his badly damaged body. His face was no longer recognizable, there was hardly a bone in his body left intact and his clothing was bloodied and torn. Such was his condition that it was not immediately evident that he had been murdered.

Working on the not unreasonable assumption that Williams had met his death as a result of a climbing accident, the local police officers had his body removed from the scene and taken to a hospital mortuary at Tremadoc, some fifteen miles away. Not until the afternoon, when his body was examined by the doctor required to certify death, was it discovered that he had been shot.

Detective Chief Superintendent Ewen Davies of the North Wales Constabulary was put in charge of the investigation. He went to the mortuary and examined the body, interviewed the police officers who had discovered it, then accompanied them back to the scene. By the time they had shown him the locations at which they had found the car and the body, it was dark and no further investigation on the spot was possible.

On the second day after the shooting Davies returned to Moel Celyn with an investigative team that included two police officers with climbing experience. They opined that, in view of the position of the body when found, Williams must have been shot whilst he was on the traverse or in the chimney. Davies had no compunction about sending them up the mountain, both were young and athletic, both members of mountain rescue teams in their off-duty time. One carried a camera, the other plastic sample bags.

Because they were inspecting the route carefully as they went, the progress of the two officers was slow, and although he understood the need for caution and careful inspection of the route, Chief Superintendent Davies chafed at the delay. They found the bullet splashes on the rock on either side of the chimney shortly after noon.

By then the killer's second victim was dead.

CHAPTER TWO

Detective Inspector Leo Wyndsor arrived at the police Weapons Training Range in Epping Forest at 9 a.m. on the day that John Williams' body was found. The heavy traffic on London's North Circular road had made the journey from his tiny bachelor flat in West Hampstead particularly frustrating and he was tired and heavy-headed from lack of sleep.

He showed his warrant card to the officer on the gate, then drove on to park outside the canteen. He parked untidily, but could not be bothered to do anything about it. Sandra was no doubt still in his bed, sleeping off the physical hangover from their shared sexual athletics that had persisted well into the early hours. It was all very well for her, he had had to get up at the crack of dawn.

Leo locked the car and walked across the tarmacadam to the door of the canteen, hands deep in the pockets of his raincoat. He stood a little over six feet and his build was slim and athletic. Blonde hair, rather longer than met with the universal approval of his senior officers, framed a rounded face in which the pale blue eyes were the dominant feature, those eyes now heavy-lidded and marked beneath with dark pouches through lack of sleep. He was beautiful rather than handsome and if his body suggested virility and strength, his face suggested a certain frailness, a vulnerability that was for most women and some men an added attraction. He was glad the target practice had been completed on the first of the two-day Advanced Course, he doubted if his hand was any too steady this morning.

The field training range had once been a World War II army camp and the original buildings, spare and inhospitable, were still in use. If the camp itself was uninviting, at least the surroundings were pleasant. Once in Epping Forest the Londoner could imagine himself in the rural heart of England instead of but a handful of miles from the urban sprawl of the city. And the trees were putting on an early autumn show, colour-turning leaves glistening with dew in the pale morning sun.

Leo was not impressed. He shivered against an imagined cold and pushed open the door of the drab sectional-built hut that now served to refresh a daily procession of officers who needed sustenance whilst they were being taught to kill. There were a dozen C.I.D. officers sitting at bare wooden tables in the room, drinking tea and coffee and chattering amongst themselves. Leo exchanged nods and words of greeting as he walked towards the self-service counter at the far end of the room. They were all of his rank and he knew them all at least by sight.

A very large West Indian lady was serving behind the stained and chipped counter. 'Tea or coffee?' she asked, favouring Leo with a wide smile.

'Is there actually any difference?' Leo asked doubtfully, eyeing the thick cups arranged in a grubby phalanx on the counter, already full with a uniformly brown and uninviting liquid.

The large lady was suddenly convulsed with laughter. 'Yes, man!' she said. 'Coffee cost you five pence more dan tea!' And so good was the joke it brought tears to her eyes. At least her good humour enlivened an otherwise thoroughly depressing room.

'Milk,' Leo ordered, smiling wanly.

He took the well-thumbed glass and sat alone at a table. An odd sense of disorientation came over him. What the hell was he doing in this dump? Surely there was a better way of earning a living. He suddenly realized that he was bored with Sandra. Beautiful as she was, the time had come for the parting of the

9

ways. He did not look forward to the almost inevitable scene, had never found the words of parting easy.

A burly Sergeant Instructor entered the room, dressed in a dark blue boiler suit, carrying a clipboard in one hand. He looked at the assembled Inspectors with a mixture of resignation and disdain. Clearly, Leo thought, here is a fellow sufferer, another man yet to discover job satisfaction.

'You'll be good enough to answer your names, gentlemen,' said Sergeant Callis, consulting his clipboard; by his tone of voice leaving no doubt that, on this course at least, rank counted for nothing.

Having satisfied himself that all were present who should be, he led them across the car park, between the prefabricated huts to a pair of huge metal doors set in a low concrete blockhouse. Inside, it smelt dank and musty and the gloom was relieved only by the yellow light of low-powered and naked electric bulbs. Concrete steps led down to a labyrinth of passages and rooms below ground level where, during the last war, the camp operations rooms had been located.

Sergeant Callis took them to a room that was cold and bare, the concrete of the walls painted a uniform dull green, the only furniture a single wooden table on which were displayed six issue .38 revolvers. He checked for the second time that morning that the weapons were empty, then addressed the assembled company.

'As I said yesterday, this course falls neatly into two halves, the offensive half and the defensive half. You spent six hours on the range yesterday and you proved you were familiar with this weapon . . .' he picked up one of the revolvers and held it up in both hands, '. . . and that you could actually hit something when you fired it, or you wouldn't be here today. Any fool can fire a gun, hitting a target is a different matter as the three who failed yesterday will tell you. Even so, what you did yesterday was the easy part. You were firing under ideal conditions, without stress, and at prefabricated targets . . . despite that, some of you blasted hell out of our poor old vicar!'

. His sally evoked a rumble of laughter and a few wry grins.

One of the tests on the range was to set the trainee fifteen yards in front of a mock-up of a house with four windows and a door. By working levers at the far end of the range the instructor made targets appear at the door or windows for a few seconds at a time. The officer had to decide if he should fire, then aim and shoot in that short space of time. One of the targets represented a man at whom the officers were entitled to shoot since he was pointing a gun at them, the others represented a woman with a child, a cripple holding a walking stick pointed outwards, and other innocents including the vicar, subject of Callis' joke. All too often the innocents were fired upon.

Callis put down the revolver, folded his arms and continued his oration. 'That was the offensive part. As police officers you are taught never to draw a gun unless you intend to use it, and if you do use it, you aim to kill. You are not taught to maim or disable, you are taught to kill. There is one small problem. In field conditions, unlike the targets we offer you here, the man you will be trying to kill will also be armed and he will probably be as anxious to kill you as you are to kill him. Most inconsiderate of him but regrettably true. Therefore, we today set about the task of trying to teach you how to kill people without getting killed yourself. That is the defensive part. Today more criminals than ever are carrying guns and are prepared to use them. A police warrant card isn't a bulletproof vest. If you don't learn the lessons we teach you here you have a good chance of ending up dead. That's a fact, ignore it at your peril. Any questions?'

There were no questions. Callis had made his point. The faces of his audience were alert and sober, he had their full attention and co-operation.

'Right,' Callis said. 'Let's see how many of you can stay alive for the next three hours.' He handed round the empty guns and led them out of the room and into the maze of corridors.

At the beginning of one corridor he stopped them and led the six officers who were armed away from the others and gave them whispered instructions. There were six doors in the bare, badly lit corridor and one of the armed officers went into each, closing the doors behind them. Callis returned to the remaining six members of the course.

'Six rooms, six armed men, one in each room,' he said. 'Your job is to go in there and either arrest them or kill them if the situation demands ... without getting killed yourself. Remember, if you kill a man who is not endangering or threatening to endanger life, yours included, the least that will happen to you is a place in the dole queue. If you don't take prompt action and the gunman intends mayhem, then you'll end up dead. You get paid to make instant decisions and be right every time. Now, go down that corridor three at a time and start earning your money. Mr Cole, Mr Wylie, Mr Wyndsor, you first. Take the first door on your left, then work your way down. When you get to the end of the corridor wait whilst the rest make their run. Right, off you go.'

Leo preceded the other two officers down the passage. When they came to the selected door Leo and Wylie took up standing positions on either side of it and Cole adopted a prone position in front of it, holding his hands forward as if he held a gun. Leo signalled to the other two, then turned the doorhandle and with a sudden movement of his body, kicked the door open and stood back out of the line of fire. The room was bare of furniture and lit by a single electric bulb. The officer playing the villain stood in the centre of the room, hands above his head. There was no sign of the gun he had been given.

'Come out,' Cole said from his position on the floor. The officer obediently walked out into the passage, his arms still above his head. Leo pushed him against the wall and began to search him as the other two held imaginary guns on their captive. Within two seconds, almost as soon as he began to search the man, Leo sensed danger. He suddenly knew that the man did not have the gun. He swung round to look into the empty room. An instructor stood in the doorway pointing the unloaded revolver at them. He had been hidden behind the door.

'Bang, bang. You're dead,' he said, smiling blandly.

'Brilliant!' shouted Sergeant Callis from the end of the passage. 'Now the poor old taxpayer has to fork out for three more widows' pensions. Just because you only see one armed man go into a room it don't mean he's the only one in there. What's more you didn't announce yourselves, didn't give him the chance to give up peaceably. If you'd managed to kill him you'd've spent the rest of your service explaining why you did it. As it is, you're dead anyway. Try the next door.'

And so it went on. At the next door the gunman took them by surprise, rushing straight at them out of a darkened room, firing as he came. At the next he refused to answer and they had to go into the bare darkened room and find him. At the next the lights were on but the room was unexpectedly furnished as a bedroom and the gunman was hidden. No two situations were the same. On no occasion did Leo and his two fellow officers do exactly the right thing. It was not intended that they should. The object of this part of the course was to show them just how hard it was to winkle an armed man out of a closed room without getting killed in the process. In that object Sergeant Callis succeeded. The officers swapped roles but none improved on the performance of the first three down what Callis casually referred to as the 'chicken run'.

By the end of the morning, however, the success rate was considerably higher and they even earned a grudging word of acknowledgement from Sergeant Callis, who was normally parsimonious with his praise. 'There's now an outside chance that you might survive if you had to do it for real,' he said, 'but I wouldn't put next month's salary cheque on it.'

They were allowed an hour for lunch. The officers blinked like startled owls as they emerged into the daylight and made their way back through the camp to the canteen.

The meal they were served did not set a new high in culinary standards. The mashed potatoes were powdery and lumpy, the Brussels sprouts were on their last legs, and as some wit in the company was quick to observe, the meat loaf gave scope for a prosecution under the Trades Descriptions Act. However, it was relatively cheap and served to occupy their gastric juices for the rest of the afternoon. Leo at least was beginning to feel a little more human.

Sergeant Callis had obviously eaten elsewhere since he did not appear in the canteen until he came to collect them for the afternoon session and then he had the look of a man who had dined pleasurably. 'On your feet, killers,' he said amiably, 'time to go.'

The sky had clouded over, the afternoon was dull and rain threatened but failed to materialize. Callis took them to a field on the outskirts of the camp which was dotted with elderly rusting cars, piles of discarded concrete blocks, the remnants of old gun emplacements, a few small tin-roofed buildings, some of which looked in imminent danger of collapse, and two partially completed brick walls.

'First of all we're going to conduct a sweep of the area,' Callis announced. 'Hidden out there are a number of instructors who've had the time of their lives dressing up as villains. Spread out ten yards apart and begin the search.'

As the line of policemen progressed across the field, with Sergeant Callis watching critically from the rear, a rough-looking figure carrying a shotgun broke from his cover behind a wall. He was instantly gunned down by the enthusiastic officers.

'You lot learned nothing,' Callis complained. 'You just shot a poor old poacher in the back and all he wanted was to escape a fine at the Magistrates' Court. Don't you blokes have no heart?'

A rifle barrel appeared from behind the corner of one of the tin buildings. It turned out to be a broom handle wielded by an instructor dressed up as a woman. The talent of Callis and his staff to create the abnormal out of the ordinary continued unabated. The line of policemen passed an innocent-looking dustbin. When they were safely past, a diminutive instructor scrambled out of the dustbin and happily gunned them down from behind.

After Callis had upbraided them, they continued. A sudden noise assailed their ears, the blasting brass of a north country band emanating from behind a pile of concrete blocks. The officers stopped in their tracks, then went forward to investigate. They found an instructor dressed as a tramp playing a tape cassette. The instructor grinned at them. Some of his teeth had

14

been painted out. When he was sure he had the attention of them all, he pointed up at the roof of a nearby building. Another instructor lay on the roof, pointing a sawn-off shotgun at them.

'Bang, bang,' he said. 'You're dead.'

'Oh, masterly performance!' said Callis caustically, coming up behind them. 'What did we say in the classroom, first hour yesterday? Never take anything for granted, never make assumptions, never allow yourself to be distracted because your life may depend on you maintaining vigilance at all times during a hunt.' He sighed theatrically. 'Let's go back and start again, shall we, gentlemen?'

This time there were no gimmicks, just briefly seen figures requiring an instant reaction, a positive reaction. The results were much better. Then they moved on to practice removing armed men from the old motor vehicles and here the officers had little to learn. It was a situation nearer to those with which they were familiar in their day-to-day work. After a spell of instruction in maintaining and making the best use of available cover, they moved on to a dugout in one corner of the field. It was simply a hole in the ground with one entrance and just about enough room inside for two people.

'For our purposes,' Sergeant Callis said, gathering the course around him, 'this here is a cellar. In this cellar is a gunman and he's got a hostage. He can't get out, you can't get in, and he's demanded a getaway car.' He pointed to one of the rusting vehicles nearby. 'There's the car if you decide to let him have it. For the purposes of this exercise you're alone, he's insane, and you've been given one minute before he kills the hostage. Right, Mr Wyndsor, what'd you do?'

Leo thought about it.

'There's no time to think,' Callis urged, 'you've got to *do* something, he's going to kill that hostage.'

'I would give him the car,' Leo said.

'Yes?' said Callis doubtfully.

'If I cannot get in and he cannot get out, then he will certainly kill the hostage in time, if the situation is as you say. It is better therefore to allow room for manoeuvre. He cannot enter the car, let alone drive it, *and* keep the hostage covered every instant.'

'You don't think so?' Callis enquired innocently. 'You'd bet the hostage's life on it, would you?'

'Yes.'

'Okay then. What next?'

'I would take cover and tackle him at a propitious moment.'

'Then?'

'Control him and search him. Hold him until assistance arrived.'

'Let's see if it works, shall we?' Callis invited. He ushered the rest of the course away from the dugout and indicated for Leo to commence.

Leo took up a position beside the entrance to the dugout and announced himself. The instructor swore at him, playing his part to the full. After a few moments of dialogue Leo agreed to make a car available, then retreated to take cover behind a wall near the vehicle.

The instructor emerged with his hostage and it was evident that he intended to make the attempt at rescue and arrest as difficult as possible. He held the hostage close to him, a gun pressed up against his victim's ear. He moved carefully to the driver's door of the car, looking round for Leo, opened it and pushed the hostage in, covering him with the gun.

There was just a brief second when, as the instructor pushed the hostage across the driver's seat and got in himself, his hand holding the gun was outside the car, pulling the door closed, and his body was inside. Leo bulleted from behind the cover of the wall and leapt feet first at the driver's door of the car, slamming it to and trapping the instructor's arm, causing him to drop his gun. Then Leo was on his feet, pulling open the car door, hauling the instructor out and forcing him face first against the side of the vehicle.

'Bloody hell! Steady on, sir,' said the instructor.

But Leo had been caught out too often during the two days of the course. He pulled the instructor's jacket down his back to pinion his arms behind him, then released his trousers, pulled them down round his ankles and began a thorough search. Leo was not squeamish. No part of the man's anatomy escaped him. He was sure that Sergeant Callis would have prepared some ingenious final twist to the situation he had set up.

Leo found the small hand gun secreted in the front of the instructor's underpants. As soon as he had done so, Sergeant Callis stepped forward. 'Okay Mr Wyndsor. That's all.'

Leo released his prisoner, who stood rubbing his bruised arm and staring balefully at him. 'Terribly sorry, old chap,' Leo said, 'but we *were* told to make it as realistic as possible.'

Callis ignored his wounded colleague, took the hand gun from Leo and showed it to the others. 'This here's a .22 automatic. Ladies' gun you might say but quite lethal at short range. I don't advise you to stick a loaded one down your trousers or you might find yourself with a high-pitched voice and a dissatisfied wife. Now, anyone got any comments on the way Mr Wyndsor dealt with this exercise?'

Detective Inspector Cole stood forward. He was short and squat, running to fat. 'It's all right for Leo to go in for that sort of athletics,' he said, 'but if I'd tried it it'd have ended up a disaster. I'd have let him go in the car and tailed him off, waited a better chance.'

'Quite right, Mr Cole,' said Callis. 'Bear in mind your own limitations. Remember you're risking other lives beside your own. Preserving life is paramount. It would have been better to let the villain get clean away than capture him at the expense of the hostage's life. Anything else?'

'Leo could have taken up a different position behind the wall,' said Wylie. 'He could have got a clear shot at the man. He was entitled to kill him because he was obviously threatening life. In fact there was less risk to the life of the hostage by killing the gunman.'

'How do you answer that, Mr Wyndsor?' Callis asked.

Leo shrugged. 'I knew what I intended to do gave me, personally, the best chance of success. As it turned out the hostage was saved and the gunman captured. If preservation of life is paramount, then that must include the gunman. We are police officers, not executioners. Killing is a very last resort.'

17

'But if it had been necessary, would you have killed him?' Callis asked.

'Yes,' Leo said. 'If there was no other way, I would have killed him.'

On the report that Sergeant Callis would submit on each officer on the course was an item headed 'Temperamental suitability to carry arms'. It simply meant, can he kill people? He asked Leo Wyndsor again: 'You sure you'd have pulled the trigger?'

Leo looked him straight in the eye. 'I'd have killed him,' he said.

Nurse James had been having trouble with her moped. It was her own fault. Not being mechanically minded she usually did not touch the machine at all, relying on the garage entirely, but she did keep a small stock of fuel at her home in case she ran out at the weekend when the garage was closed. The previous Sunday she had filled the tank herself and had made up the wrong petrol–oil mixture. As a result the single plug had taken to oiling up, making starting difficult and progress uncertain.

To make matters worse, her schedule of house calls had been so heavy since the Sunday that she had had no opportunity to have the simple fault corrected. It seemed that half the women in the neighbourhood must have been touched by the madness of spring that year, so many of them were pregnant.

On the second day after the death of John Williams, Nurse James rode uncertainly along the high and lonely road between Penmachno and Yspyty Ifan, heading for an isolated farmhouse. Her machine was trailing black smoke and firing intermittently so that her progress was slow and spasmodic. Finally the moped stopped altogether. Fortunately the weather was mild and although the sky was overcast, it was not raining. She put the machine up on to its stand and sat on it, fuming as she considered whether to wait for a passing car or begin to walk.

After ten minutes John Jones, a local hill farmer, stopped in his battered Landrover and after the usual slow and friendly exchange of pleasantries and commiserations, took out the offending plug, cleaned it and started the moped for her. She thanked him profusely and continued on her way.

It would have been better for Nurse James if John Jones had ignored her, driven on, rendered her no assistance, left her to walk back the way she had come.

Up ahead on the lonely road, the killer waited.

CHAPTER THREE

He had travelled during the night and had used the dull light of early dawn to select his hiding place, a hump of land topped by a scattering of rocks, conveniently sited beside the Penmachno to Yspyty Ifan road.

He was some way from his base and this was a matter of deliberate policy. He was aware of the danger of killing too near his home or selecting venues uniform enough to reveal a pattern and allow any investigating officer an educated guess at the location of his base. He was not so insane that he did not realize that he was already being hunted, nor did he underestimate the police. He knew that the biggest risk he faced was that his base be found and he had gone to considerable lengths to ensure security. Once free, up in the mountains and valleys, he was invulnerable. No man would catch him, see him even, and if anyone came too close, they begged their own death.

If he had a weakness it was his extreme self-confidence, amounting almost to an arrogant assumption of superiority in his chosen field, or perhaps his obsessive enthusiasm for the high-performance target rifle and what it could achieve in the hands of an expert shot. If these were indeed weaknesses they were weaknesses of which he was unaware and, in any event, they were as likely to act for him as against him.

He had weighed up and decided to accept the extra risks of

killing on a public road for the overriding reason that it provided
a very special test of his rifle and his skill. His target would be
moving at speed towards or away from him, lengthening or closing the range by a factor he would not be able to compute
exactly. Also, since there would be no suitable background, he
would not be able to see the fall of shot should he miss. It was
typical of him that, since he had been dissatisfied with his first
shoot on Moel Celyn, he should now choose a more difficult
target rather than an easier one.

After he had chosen his hiding place the killer made himself
comfortable, placing a small groundsheet on the coarse damp
grass, changing its position until he was satisfied that when he
came to shoot he would be at the best angle to the road and that
no lumpy rocks beneath would irritate him, causing loss of concentration.

For a long while after dawn he watched the sparse traffic on
the road, concerned with selecting a suitable target. It was not
enough simply to put a shot through the windscreen of a car or
van or lorry. It was important that he be sure that it was his shot
which killed and not the subsequent crash of the motor vehicle.
He wanted plain evidence of his own expertise, he was not
interested in killing dramatically, only in killing efficiently and
skilfully.

The problem was solved for him after an hour or so of watching. A young man appeared over the brow of the hill behind him,
bent low over the handlebars of a powerful motor-cycle, travelling at speed, handling the machine with more than average skill.
The killer watched him but did not move, knowing that the
motor-cyclist would be out of sight long before he could prepare
himself for the shot. But when the harsh noise of the engine had
receded into the distance towards Penmachno, he began to
unpack his rifle.

The motor-cyclist had presented an idea target. Perhaps he
would return, if not that day the next. The killer had food and
water with him and had infinite patience. Or perhaps another
motor-cyclist would come later that day. Now that his mind was
made up, he could prepare himself, make ready for the shot.

He took the rifle from its carrying case and fitted the scopesight. Both rifle and scopesight were wrapped with camouflage material, matching his jacket, and strips of the material hung down from the rifle giving it a totally inaccurate appearance of untidiness and neglect. He eased himself into position, wrapped the padded sling tight round his left arm, pulled the butt hard into his shoulder and looked through the sight.

Although it was now full light the sky was heavily clouded and visibility poor. He was glad of the scopesight because although he was aware that it would not make him or the rifle more accurate, it would be especially valuable this day for its light-gathering power and the good contrast it offered. He decided to shoot at a range of 400 yards, any less and the test was not severe enough for his liking, any more and his chance of success with the single shot he intended to allow himself rapidly diminished. He set the scopesight, then looked through it again, picking out a spot on the road that he estimated to be about 400 yards from his position, conveniently marked by a small white-faced rock at the side of the narrow, pathless road.

The killer adjusted the sight many times in the next hour, as the clouds became heavier and the light worse. He was still not entirely satisfied when he heard the distant sound of Nurse James' moped approaching from Penmachno, but he decided that this motor-cyclist would be his target.

He took a single bullet from the breast pocket of his jacket, where it had been kept comfortably warm, loaded it straight into the breech of the rifle, forced it home with the bolt action, then took a sight on the white-faced stone that was his marker, holding the rubber ring of the scopesight tight round his eye to exclude extraneous light.

Then the moped was in sight, the rider hunched forward over the handlebars in an awkward posture, as if nervous and uncertain of the machine. The killer heard the sick note of the engine and calculated that despite whatever fault it had, the moped was approaching him at not less than thirty miles per hour. He made rapid calculations in his head and settled himself to the shot, willing his body to total stillness, concentrating utterly on the task at hand.

His right forefinger curled round the trigger and took up first pressure as he picked up the moped in the sight and travelled with it towards his marker. He squeezed on the trigger as if it were a sponge, with firm but gentle and progressive pressure.

The bullet struck Nurse James just below her left breast, passed through the lower section of her heart and exited in the small of her back, leaving a gaping wound. She died instantly. The force of the bullet threw her sideways and backwards off her machine and her body skidded across the road and lay in an untidy heap amongst the coarse grass and scattered stones at the roadside. The machine toppled over, the front wheel turned sideways on and sparks flew as it skated across the tarmac, the engine still turning, coughing out black smoke. Then the moped ground to a stop, the engine died, and there was silence.

The killer watched through the scopesight. He felt a thrill of pleasure and excitement. When the rider's body had bucketed backwards off the machine it told him that he had made a successful body shot. No, not merely a successful shot, a quite superb shot under most exacting conditions. The kind of shot of which any marksman could be proud.

He smiled in self-congratulation as he removed the scopesight; and he kissed the warm wood of the butt before he packed the rifle away in its camouflaged carrying case.

Detective Chief Superintendent Bob Staunton and Detective Inspector Leo Wyndsor were together in Staunton's office on the third floor of the Scotland Yard building in Victoria Street, London.

It was mid-morning on the Saturday, four days after the murder of Nurse James in the mountains of North Wales. Both officers knew of her death and that of the climber, they both kept a professional eye on the daily papers, but as the days passed and other events took the headlines their interest waned.

They were part of C.I. Department's murder squad and in the

parlance of that *élite* band they were 'Number One', top of the list of paired officers to be called upon should the Metropolitan Police receive a request from another force for assistance. They had held that position for nearly a month and murders had come and gone in the provinces but no Chief Constable had sought their aid. The waiting was tedious since they could not take on any cases which would prevent them from leaving London immediately or which would require them to return to London to attend court once they had commenced work on a murder enquiry. Time hung heavy on their hands and they were chained to the office, having to report their whereabouts even when they were off duty so that they could be contacted instantly. After a month it told on the nerves and they had got to the state where they jumped every time the telephone rang.

They were drinking tea from thick white cups and chatting in desultory fashion, in the relaxed manner of old friends. Yet on the face of it they were a disparate pair. Bob Staunton would not see fifty again, he was short and heavily built with a bull neck, heavy features and a shock of wiry black hair greying at the temples. He spoke with the sharp accent of the Londoner born and bred and his manner was blunt and uncompromising. He looked an unlikely candidate for the role of Britain's most successful murder investigator, yet that was exactly his position.

Leo Wyndsor was more than twenty years his junior, the epitome of young upper-middle-class manhood. His accent, his manner of dress, his ambience of certainty, his casual assumption of authority bespoke his privileged upbringing. Yet he was not all that he seemed. He suffered, as did many of his age and background, from a deep-rooted sense of guilt centred on a colonial history in which he had played no part and in the injustice of the now all-but-defunct class system that had made him what he was. He was plagued by a carping, critical alter ego which mocked his achievements and gloried in his defeats.

Unlike Bob Staunton, who was never troubled by doubts about his motives and capabilities and who was regarded by all with affection, Leo Wyndsor was not universally liked. Many of his contemporaries were offended as much by his outstanding academic ability and flair for detective work as by his good looks and resultant success with the fair sex, and many of his senior officers considered him arrogant and sometimes contemptuous of authority.

The undoubted friendship between the two men was a constant surprise to all. It subsisted because Bob Staunton could read Leo like a book, saw through his façade, and knew that he had the potential to become an outstanding detective and achieve high rank provided that he, Bob, had the training of him for a few years, had the chance to educate him in the real world of people, in the university of life. For Leo's part, he recognized in Bob Staunton the granite certainty he himself lacked, despite appearance, and a peasant shrewdness that more than made up for any educational defects. Bob Staunton was a hard case, a man's man, and if he lacked flair and intuition, he made up for it with dogged determination and endless patience.

As an investigative team they were well matched, complementing each other, trusting each other, reliant on each other, each with a healthy regard for the other's abilities. They were teamed together now by mutual choice, as they had been often before, a choice based as much on affection as on professional admiration. And although neither would have dreamt of using the word 'love' in describing their relationship, none the less a better word would be hard to find.

Bob Staunton slurped noisily at his tea, his chair turned away from the desk so that he could stare aimlessly out of the double-glazed and permanently fixed window of his office at the hurrying traffic in Victoria Street. Conversation had lapsed into a companionable silence. They both jumped when the telephone rang.

'That's the phone,' Bob said, making no move to answer it.

Leo picked up the receiver. 'Chief Superintendent Staunton's office,' he said, grinning as Bob noiselessly imitated his Oxbridge accent.

'Is that you, Wyndsor?'

Leo recognized the voice. 'Yes, sir.'

'Mr Staunton there?'

'Yes, sir.'

'Both of you, my office, five minutes.'

'Yes, sir.' Leo replaced the receiver.

'Don't tell me,' Bob said, 'that was Sir.'

'The A.C.C. presents his compliments and requests the pleasure of our company in his office in five minutes.'

'If I know Bernie, he didn't use them words.'

Leo grinned. 'He's not exactly verbose.'

Bob replaced his cup on the desk, ignoring the saucer, and picked thoughtfully at his nose. 'Reckon he's got business for us?' he asked.

Bernard Brightwell, Assistant Commissioner Crime, was a short, slightly built man with an almost entirely bald head and a permanently worried expression which had left indelible lines across his forehead. He waved his visitors to chairs and shuffled amongst the piles of paper on his desk.

'Telephone call,' he said. 'Chief Constable North Wales. Two shootings. Know about it?'

'First was a climber, second a nurse,' said Bob, catching Brightwell's abrupt manner of speech.

'Yes.' Brightwell came up with a single sheet of memo paper. 'Requests assistance. Not the usual sort though. Wants us to provide an experienced undercover team.'

'You mean we wouldn't be in charge of the job?' Bob asked.

'No. Not exactly. Get a free hand though. No interference.'

'You've agreed then?'

'Yes. You don't want the job?'

'I didn't say that, sir. You know what it's like. Some of these provincial lads don't like us blokes from down here in the smoke pokin' our noses in. Can get awkward if you're not officially in charge, know what I mean?'

'Doesn't arise. Chief Superintendent Davies asked for you. I can get another team.'

'I never turned down a job in me life.'

'Good. Leave tomorrow morning.'

'Where for?'

'Bangor. Davies will pick you up, brief you. After that, you're on your own.'

Bob Staunton stood and Leo followed suit. Bob hesitated on his way to the door. 'I suppose you know, this sort of job, it's bound to be expensive, I mean, bound to cost, ain't it?'

Brightwell sighed. 'You're always expensive, Bob,' he said.

'Me?' said Bob indignantly. 'Cheapest copper in the world, me!'

Brightwell looked pained. Leo stifled a grin as he held the door open for Bob to leave. Staunton might be brilliant, but he certainly did not come cheap.

They returned to Bob's office. He unlocked a drawer in his desk and produced a bottle of whisky and two almost clean glasses.

'Too early for me,' Leo said.

'Sun's up, ain't it?' said Bob. 'Get it down you. Do you good. Celebration.'

He handed over a glass. Leo took it resignedly. 'I hear you've caught Brightwell's disease,' he said, straightfaced.

'Eh?'

'The parsimonious use of the English language.'

'Oh, that. Yeah, it's catching all right, but I'll get over it. What d'you make of this job then?'

'Sounds rather interesting. At least if we are going incognito I'll not have to toil all the way to North Wales with that cumbersome murder bag.'

'No interest in the job, that's your trouble, mate. Tell you what, I don't like the sound of it.'

'Why not?'

'You read the papers. No motive. When you got no motive, no lead, then you're in bother.'

'I imagine they'd not have asked for us but for the fact that they were in difficulty.'

'True. Very true.'

Leo smiled to himself as he sipped at his drink. It had become almost a ritual that Bob Staunton expressed the gravest doubts about their chance of success before they set out on an enquiry, and then, once they had started work, became adamantly certain of an arrest against all odds.

27

'I'm going home,' Bob said suddenly. 'Ring this . . . what's 'is name?'

'Davies,' Leo supplied.

'That's him. Ring Davies and tell him when we'll be there. Then give me a ring at home when you've got the train times, okay?'

'Very well.'

Bob marked the level of the whisky in the bottle with a ball-point pen before replacing it in the cupboard and locking the cupboard securely.

'Expecting burglars, sir?' Leo enquired blandly.

'Yes, mate. Bottle bandits.'

'Surely not.'

'It's that Alfie Westmore. I've got his number, sussed him out years ago.'

'Mr Westmore? He's a personal friend of yours, is he not?'

'So he might be. He's also a bottle bandit. When Alfie gets the taste there ain't a bottle what's safe.'

'But he wouldn't take anything from your personal cupboard . . . would he? I mean, fellow Chief Superintendents and all that?'

'Listen, mate. Rank don't have nothin' to do with it, nor does bein' friends. Once a bottle bandit, always a bottle bandit, stand on me.'

Leo sighed heavily. 'Another illusion shattered!'

Bob paused at the door, one finger to his temple, as if a thought had just come to him. 'Leo . . . important job, mate.'

Leo fell for it, as he always did. 'Yes?'

'Don't forget to wash the glasses.'

Bob roused his driver out of the rest-room and was driven home to his tiny box-like semi-detached house in West Ham. He could long ago have afforded to move to a larger, more opulent house in one of the outer suburbs but he preferred to remain where he was, amongst people he knew, in an area where he felt at home. He had no pretensions, no social ambitions, and he pitied those who had.

He would spend his day pottering in his toy garden, tinkering with the modest family saloon, telephoning his children and grandchildren to say goodbye. Then, in the evening, sit in his comfortable chair beside his comfortable wife with a glass of whisky to hand and watch bland and undemanding television programmes. In the morning he and his wife would share a small glass of sherry and exchange slightly embarrassed hugs before he left to enter that other world in which his wife could play no part. She would worry about him, pray secretly for his safe return, but say nothing of her fears, knowing that once he left the house he would have little time to think of her, would have burdens enough without her adding to them.

They had a relationship that was strong and durable, honed by the years and by shared experience. From this sound base Bob Staunton went out into his complex, demanding and sometimes dangerous world armed with confidence and energy.

Once Bob had left him, Leo Wyndsor set about the business of organizing their journey to Wales. He checked the train times, arranged for them to be met at Bangor, then telephoned Bob. Afterwards he emptied his desk of current files and correspondence and locked it, handing the paperwork over to his Chief Inspector.

His next call was to the clerk's office where he collected cash from the imprest fund and travel warrants for the journey. This was not achieved without dispute. The elderly senior clerk took his function as part controller of the public purse with extreme seriousness and harboured dark suspicions about the way in which certain officers, Leo Wyndsor certainly included, spent the money entrusted to them. The fact that Leo would have to account on paper for every single penny he spent during the enquiry did not weigh with the clerk. Who could keep track of what was or was not spent on informants? A nasty loophole in the police fiscal arrangements was this business of paying informants. If he had his way . . .

Leo settled for rather less than he would have liked and a good deal more than pleased the clerk. Having booked himself and

Bob Staunton out in their respective duty books he said a short round of farewells and caught a taxi home.

When he entered his flat he found Sandra, dressed only in one of his dressing-gowns, sprawled in a chair watching television. As he passed the kitchen he saw that it was littered with dirty crockery. Sandra's Swiss finishing school had not included washing-up in its curriculum.

She got languidly to her feet, switched off the television and came to him, winding her arms round his neck and kissing him on the lips. The dressing-gown fell open and she did not bother to cover herself.

'You're home early, lover,' she said.

'I shall be going away in the morning.'

'Oh, poop! How long for?'

'I'm not sure. Several weeks anyway.'

'I don't know why you bother. You could do better.'

'It pays the bills.'

She kissed him again, but without passion. 'Want some coffee?' she asked.

Leo shook his head. She had become shallow and boring, there would be no better time to end the relationship. But she was beautiful, and her naked body stirred him.

'Take me to bed, then,' she said.

She left later that evening. Leo never did get around to telling her that the affair was over.

Bob and Leo left London late on Sunday morning and after an uneventful journey were met at Bangor by a smart, young plain-clothes officer who introduced himself as Detective Sergeant Gwyn Richards. Richards ushered them into a battered old saloon car and swept them out of the town with a brisk efficiency that left them slightly breathless.

'Know much about this job, son?' Bob enquired when he had settled into his seat.

'Very little, sir. I've only been on the murder enquiry for a few days . . . since the second killing when we enlarged the squad.'

'Where're we goin' then?' Bob asked.

'Murder H.Q. at Portmadoc, sir. It's not a long ride, but if you want to stop to eat or anything, let me know.'

'No need to stop, mate,' Bob said. 'You just show this dog the rabbit fast as you like.'

Soon after leaving Bangor the road began to rise steeply and beyond Bethesda they were into the mountain heart of North Wales. There were times when the old car seemed most reluctant, slowing to crawling pace near the top of some of the inclines.

'You sure this heap'll make it?' Bob enquired anxiously.

Richards grinned back over his shoulder. 'She'll make it, sir, don't you worry. Used to it she is, see.'

Bob accepted Richards' assurance with a doubtful grunt and stared out of the side window. There was little to be seen since the sky was heavily clouded and dusk had come early. On their left was a sheer granite face where the road had been blasted out of the side of the mountain, on their right a drop beyond a drystone wall into a misty and shadowed valley.

It was fully dark by the time Sergeant Richards drove into Portmadoc and at the sight of people, buildings, and neon lighting Bob Staunton brightened a little. He was a man of the city. Open countryside offended and depressed him.

Richards drove into a yard behind a substantial stone building and a pair of tall wooden doors were closed behind them. 'Here we are, sir,' Richards said. 'The incident room is on the first floor, the ground floor is the National Insurance offices. There was a bit of a row, but we managed to keep this car park for ourselves.'

'I should bloody well hope so,' said Bob. 'Thanks for the ride.'

Detective Chief Superintendent Davies came across from the rear of the building to greet them. He introduced himself and led them up an iron staircase on the outside of the rear of the building, up to the first floor. He was a smartly dressed man despite his bulk and short stature and his voice was deep and melodious, his Welsh accent suggested rather than actual. His dark hair was thick and heavy and he had large brown eyes set in a well rounded face below which was a substantial double chin. He looked like a

31

prosperous dormouse, fattened up and ready for winter hibernation.

As they mounted the stairs he said: 'The Chief Constable's here, Mr MacCready, wanted to see you at once. You'll like Mr MacCready, not a bad sort . . .'

'You've seen one Chief Constable you've seen 'em all,' said Bob. 'There ain't nothing he can tell us you can't, I'll bet.'

'Perhaps so. But it's politics, see. This job is bad news for him.'

'Oh yeah,' Bob said. 'Know all about that, don't we. Don't suppose he brought a bottle of Scotch?'

'I don't think so.'

'No,' said Bob sadly, 'they never do.'

Davies led them into the building, along a bare, neon-lit corridor and into a small functionally furnished room where Chief Constable Alex MacCready sat at a desk. He came as something of a surprise to the two London officers. He was in his late forties, slimly built and looked to be in fair physical shape. He was neatly but not expensively dressed, his hair and moustache black but greying slightly, and he wore heavy horn-rimmed glasses. He had the appearance of a moderately successful insurance agent or a middle level civil servant. He stood to greet the newcomers and when he spoke his voice was without accent, his use of words careful and considered.

'Welcome, gentlemen. I know you both by reputation. Glad to have you with us.'

Bob and Leo shook hands and took chairs at the Chief Constable's invitation. Something clicked in Bob Staunton's mind. He knew who this man was now, he had read about him in the *Police Review*. MacCready had come up through the ranks the hard way, spending ten years in the C.I.D. in the slums of Glasgow, where he had been born. He was no boy wonder. Along the way he had collected a handful of awards for bravery and had qualified as a barrister. Alex MacCready was not a man to take at face value.

'Pleasure to work with you, sir,' Bob said.

32

'We have a nasty one here, Bob,' MacCready said. 'There's no connection between the two dead people and I doubt if there's any connection between either of them and the murderer. It looks as though we have a maniac who kills for the love of it. You know what that means . . .'

'Yes. A lot of bloody hard work,' said Bob.

'Exactly. Now, there were two reasons why we asked you to come. First, for reasons which Ewen . . .' he indicated Chief Superintendent Davies, '. . . will explain in a moment, we believe this man is local, and second, following on from that really, we felt we needed a couple of experienced murder investigators out on the ground. People who could get around the pubs, hotels, small shops and so forth without any fear of being recognized as policemen and who would know instantly if a word of gossip was of real value to us. Our own men have done the round of their informants and come up with nothing. We think the killer may not have a record. We do, however, know two things about him. He is a psychopath and he is also an international class shot.'

'How do we know that for certain, sir?' Leo asked.

'Ewen will explain in a moment, Leo. The point is, you both know what to look for, what sort of questions to ask to unearth someone like that. He's here, and in a fairly limited and sparsely populated area, as you'll see on the map next door. I suggest you find a hotel for tonight at Betws-y-coed, then split up and work the area after that as you see fit. You'll have no contact with this office unless you wish it but Ewen will give you any help you need. You'll have the telephone numbers here, my office number and my home number. Call me any time of the day or night. Ewen will take you next door now and brief you properly, then I suggest we adjourn to a hostelry I know and have a meal and a drop of something while we have a final chat.'

Bob hauled himself to his feet. 'Sir,' he said, 'you're a gentleman. We'll do that.'

MacCready smiled briefly. 'I've been accused of many things in my time, Bob,' he said, 'but never of being a gentleman!'

Davies led them back into the corridor, then to a large room which had been taken over as the incident centre. As soon as he opened the door they were met by the chattering of typewriters, the ringing of telephones and the clatter of voices.

Leo cast a professional eye over the layout. The centre of the room was occupied by banks of filing cabinets with small drawers, housing the cross-reference card index system that is the hub of the investigative system employed by most British police forces. Information from statements, informants, telephone messages and local knowledge is collected, collated, transferred to index cards, the cards cross-referenced, then filed so that no single item of information however insignificant is lost. Apart from the main index, there are sub-indexes dealing with motor vehicles coming to notice as a result of the enquiry, with suggested suspects, with public houses, with weapons, with forensic, ballistic and medical reports, and a host of others. It is a kind of hand-operated computer for collecting, separating, storing and disseminating information and it is an invaluable investigative tool.

Along one wall was a line of desks, each with a telephone, along another a photo-copying machine and a bank of metal cupboards for storing exhibits. At the head of the room was a large desk at which sat a stolid-looking uniformed Chief Inspector and an officer of presumably equal rank who, but for the fact that he wore civilian clothes, might have been his twin. There were about fifteen other officers at work in the room, men and women, and there was a general air of intense purpose and efficient application. Leo Wyndsor, who had set up and run many such incident rooms, was considerably impressed.

A series of large-scale maps of the area had been posted on one wall and it was to these that Chief Superintendent Davies led them, followed by the discreetly inquisitive eyes of the officers in the room.

'This one here,' said Davies, 'just marks the venues of the two killings. The first was here, near this lake, Llyn Celyn . . .'

'That was the climber?' Bob put in.

'Yes. Young chap, name of Williams. Schoolteacher, single man, climbed as a hobby, came from Newport. Second one was here, on the Penmachno to Yspyty Ifan road. Local nurse, mid-wife, shot off her moped, killed instantly.'

'Same gun used for both?' Leo asked.

'Yes. We had a hell of a job to find the second bullet, it passed right through the nurse's body, shorter range we think. Anyway, the rifling on the bullet is the same as on the one that killed Williams.'

'What sort of ammo was it?' Bob asked.

'Interesting that,' Davies said, scratching reflectively at his double chin, 'it's 7.62 mm NATO ammunition, not made here, made in Belgium. It's standard British army issue but at the moment they're not admitting to being short of any.'

'It's easy enough to get hold of guns and ammo these days,' Bob commented.

'Do we know anything about the rifle?' Leo asked.

'Yes. The ballistics boys had a field day . . . let me show you some photographs . . .'

Davies walked away to collect a folder from a nearby table. When he returned he opened it out and flicked through the numbered photographs. 'This first lot are Williams' body, so smashed up you can hardly see anything . . . but here, if you see, there's the entrance wound in his back, and . . . on this one . . .' he turned over several pages, '. . . here, this is the rock face where he was standing. It's a chimney, going almost straight up, just a cleft in the rock really, see these marks? . . . these were the first two shots . . .'

'He missed then . . .' Bob began.

'No. The experts tell me they're sure they were sighting shots. What's more, they were able to work out where the killer was placed when he fired . . . depth of penetration of the bullet and the angle it entered the body, understand? Anyway, we found the place . . . here's a photo. Handy spot.'

'What was the range?' Leo asked.

'Near as dammit 800 yards.'

'That makes him a world-class shot does it, killing someone at that range?' Bob asked.

'More to it than that,' Davies said. 'There's the fact he picked his spot to fire from to give himself the ideal angle of fire, then took careful sighting shots. Then there's what he did the second time . . . look at these . . .' He pushed the first folder of photographs aside and opened another marked 'Murder of Gwyneth James'. 'That's the body . . . this is where he was, 400 yards away. As far as we can tell he hit a moving target, probably doing between twenty and thirty miles an hour. That, the experts tell me, makes him either dead lucky or a top-class shot . . . and I don't happen to think it was luck.'

'Reckon you're right, Ewen mate,' said Bob.

'And the rifle, sir?' Leo asked.

'Oh yes, the rifle. Well, they reckon it's probably something special. A target rifle, used for competition shooting, probably fitted with a telescopic sight . . . a rather unusual piece of hardware . . . and incidentally, most of these target rifles fire 7.62 mm military cartridges.'

'But that's a guess, it being a target rifle?' Leo asked.

'Yes. But it's a good one in all the circumstances.'

'Obviously you've circulated all the rifle clubs and suchlike then?' Bob asked.

'Yes. Every single one in the U.K. Hell of a job. We've also got a list of names and addresses of all registered members. We're in the process of seeing them all and taking statements. Got to be done even though I'm sure he's local.'

'Nothing so far?' Bob enquired.

'No rifles stolen. All we have is a carrying case for a target rifle stolen from near Plymouth. I've got photographs of a similar case . . .'

'Anything to suggest our man nicked it?' Bob asked.

'No. But if it *was* him he already had the rifle because when he stole the carrying case he left a similar rifle untouched.'

'There are no likely suspects in a local club?' Leo enquired.

'No. We've been through them with a fine comb. I can't be sure it isn't one of them of course . . . you can never be sure.'

'What I don't understand,' Leo said, 'is if our man is local, why should he go as far as Plymouth to steal a carrying case?

36

Presumably they would be available much nearer home, at the houses of the local club members.'

Davies raised his hand in a helpless gesture. His double chin wobbled above a perfect white collar. 'Ask me another. Perhaps it wasn't our man at all.'

'Why's he local, Ewen?' Bob asked. 'I mean, you say he's local, why d'you think that?'

'No reason.' He patted his ample stomach. 'I feel it in here,' he said, 'gut feeling. The Chief Constable thinks the same. You get two jobs like this, close by each other, the killer's never that far away, is he?'

Bob Staunton grunted a reluctant acknowledgement of this truism. But he preferred hard facts to intuition every time and this seemed likely to turn out to be one of those cases where hard facts were at a premium. 'How big an area're we supposed to cover?' he asked.

Davies referred them to a map on the wall. 'I think you could cover this area bounded by the roads between Ffestiniog, Betws-y-coed, Bala, back to Trawsfynydd and Ffestiniog.'

'Looks like a lot of bloody mountains to me,' said Bob.

'That's right. It'll make your job a little easier. More mountains, less people. D'you want guns?'

Bob shook his head vehemently. 'No thanks, mate. Bloody dangerous things, guns.'

'They're here if you want them. We have .38 and .45 revolvers and a few rifles, just in case.'

'We're here to nick a murderer,' Bob said, 'not to start the third world war.'

Davies shrugged. 'As you wish. If there's nothing else, we can go back to my office. I've prepared maps for you, and marked the murder sites. You might want to look at the sites some time. D'you want to see the bodies?'

'No thanks. Seen enough of them.'

'Right. I'll give you the car keys as well. There's a car each for you, we put them in the municipal car park. I'll drop you off there after we've had a meal, then you're on your own. What cover will you use?'

37

'Hadn't thought about it,' Bob said.

'There's still plenty of tourists around, up to the end of September anyway. If you don't fancy climbing perhaps you could be birdwatching, quite a lot of that goes on here.'

Bob grinned. 'Goes on everywhere, mate. Don't worry about it, we'll think of somethin'. We'd best get a move on or Alex MacCready might change his mind about buyin' us a drink.'

The killer consulted his map. He had been out spotting that day and had chanced upon an ideal target, a target that would test not only his rifle and his shooting skill but also his fieldcraft. The only doubt in his mind was whether he could afford to kill so close to his base or whether he should look for a similar target further afield.

One of the candles guttered out, and the stygian darkness that surrounded him crept a little closer. He took a new candle from his pack, lit it from another and set it in place in the pool of soft wax in the old saucer. The added light pushed back the shadows and illuminated the map.

Three miles was closer than he would have liked, yet far enough to ensure that no random search would find him. The police might well suppose that he would not operate so close to his base. That was a reasonable assumption for them to make. He marked on the map the places where he had already killed and the place where he proposed to kill next, then studied them. By no system of logic or mathematics could his home be discovered by reference to the venue of the killings, only by chance. All that could be told was that three people had been shot dead by the same gun and within less than ten miles of each other. He no longer asked if he should make the shot, he had already decided. The element of risk was essential, it added flavour to the shoot.

After a while he put out the candles and was soon asleep. He did not dream. He slept soundly. He was never afflicted by guilt or remorse.

A target, after all, is just a target.

CHAPTER FOUR

Having partaken of an excellent meal and rather more modestly of an excellent bottle of Glenfiddich at the Chief Constable's expense, Bob and Leo were driven to the municipal car park where Chief Superintendent Davies identified the vehicles he had provided for them and left them to their own devices.

The conversation over the meal had not enlightened them to any greater extent in respect of their task. They had a free hand as to how they conducted their investigation, but very little to go on. No one, not even the victims, probably, had ever set eyes on the killer and there was not a shred of evidence available, except educated conjecture based on his ability to shoot well, to identify him. Even so, a good meal, a measure of his favourite liquid refreshment and a sight of concrete and tarmac had cheered Bob Staunton considerably. Like a trained hound at the start of a hunt he radiated eagerness and confidence.

Leo kept his doubts to himself. So far as he could see they were hunting a wraith. Never had he been involved in a murder enquiry where so little could initially be deduced about the murderer, where there was such a paucity of facts upon which to base a line of enquiry. They were being sent out to track down an insane killer but were blinded and crippled by lack of information.

Leo led the way and took the road out of Portmadoc that led

through the Vale of Ffestiniog, driving slowly so that Bob, never the most competent of drivers, should have the opportunity to get used to the controls of the strange vehicle. They climbed up through Blaenau Ffestiniog in total darkness, seeing nothing but the road ahead illuminated by the beams of their headlights once the town was left behind.

When they had passed Dolwyddelan, the road began to drop slowly down into the Conway valley and joined the road from Llangollen just outside Betws-y-coed. After some confusion in the town, Leo found the way to the motel Chief Constable Mac-Cready had recommended. It lay in several acres of lush valley fields bordering the River Conway, the modern buildings looking painfully out of place in this rural setting. Bob and Leo booked in under their own names and were shown to adjacent terraced chalets in one of the aesthetically uninspiring blocks that squatted round the main service building, to which the chalets were so clearly related by the arid genetics of cost effective architecture.

The rooms were identical, totally uninviting in their clinical cleanliness and the regimental order of the provision of amenities. On the back of the door, preserved behind a clear plastic sheet framed in an imitation wood frame, was a forbidding list of orders and instructions, a sharp reminder to the insensitive that this was no home.

Half an hour after they arrived Bob Staunton walked into Leo's room, a plastic tooth glass in his hand. 'Got any gargle, son?' he asked hopefully.

Leo took a bottle of Glenfiddich from his case, poured Bob a stiff tot, then collected his own glass from the minute bathroom and did the same for himself. Bob took possession of the only armchair, so Leo sat on the bed. Bob sipped thoughtfully at his drink before opening the conversation.

'What're we goin' to be?' he asked.

'Be?' Leo enquired.

'Yeah.'

'Oh, yes . . . I thought freelance newspaper reporters, since we'll be asking so many questions.'

40

'Not bad. I'll buy that. Get the map out, we'll sort out who's goin' where.'

Leo spread out on the bed one of the maps Chief Superintendent Davies had supplied them with and they consulted it in silence for a moment.

'This road here,' Bob said. 'The . . . B4407 . . . more or less cuts our area in two, east to west. You take the north half, I'll take the south, okay?'

'As you wish. Perhaps I had best come with you in the morning . . . at least until you have settled your lodgings, otherwise I won't know where you are.'

'No need, mate. Use your brains. All we do is call Ewen Davies when we're settled and leave him the phone number and address. He'll tell you where I am. Call me tomorrow night.'

Leo folded up the map and put it away. 'You have your copy of the map?' he asked.

'Yeah. Don't bother. I won't get lost.' Bob finished his drink at a gulp. 'Dry old pub this,' he commented.

Leo refilled his glass. 'We have a great deal of ground to cover,' he said. 'How do you intend to go about it?'

'One thing I'm not doin',' said Bob emphatically, 'is leapin' up and down mountains, bloody fool's game that. And sheep don't make good informants. Put yourself about, son, meet people, buy drinks, get yourself in, that's the way. If he's local we'll pick up a sniff sooner or later.'

'It may be later rather than sooner. It will take months to cover every town and village in our area properly.'

'No need. We don't have to. You know what it's like, a place like this. Everyone knows everyone for miles around, most of them'll be related. Biggest place is Ffestiniog and that ain't exactly a metropolis.'

'Always provided of course that he is local. He just might not be.'

'Don't be a bloody misery. He ain't no tourist. He picked his spots. He knows this place better'n I know the saloon bar of me local boozer.'

Leo sipped his drink. 'Yes. You're right of course. I was just

41

pointing out that we have no firm evidence that he's a local. Even allowing that he is, it will be no easy task to locate him unless he makes a slip.'

'He's a nutter. Got to be. So he ain't suddenly got that way, it don't happen overnight. So someone knows him, knows about him. Maybe a lot of people do. We've got chances.'

'The problem is,' Leo said, 'he will almost certainly kill again before we get to him.'

'Oh, yeah,' Bob agreed. 'Some other poor bastard is goin' to get topped. He won't give over till we feel his collar, that's for sure.' Bob looked thoughtfully at his empty glass. 'You know, I reckon I could manage another drop,' he said, 'since you're so bloody mean pourin' it out.'

They met for breakfast in the dining-room the following morning. Bob complained loudly to Leo about the quality and quantity of the food but still managed to pack away enough for two.

When Leo had booked out of the hotel and settled the account, he gave Bob half the cash he had drawn from the imprest fund at Scotland Yard and brought both their cases down to the cars.

'Good luck, son,' Bob said. 'Stay out of strange beds.'

Leo grinned. 'I suspect my social life may be somewhat limited for the next few weeks,' he said, getting into the car.

'I know you,' Bob said with mock censure. 'You'd find skirt on the moon, just keep your mind on the job.'

'I never think of anything else,' Leo replied.

Bob watched Leo drive away, then got into his own car and followed him down the road. He could with confidence leave Leo Wyndsor to get on with his part of the job and concentrate on what he himself intended. The cars separated just outside Betws-y-coed and Bob took the main road as far as Pentrefoelas, then turned off towards Bala. He had no intention of ending up in a farmhouse miles from anywhere, or in yet another plastic rabbit hutch like the one they had just left. He had definite ideas about accommodation and these ideas included a bar with flexible opening hours, food of sensible quantity and basic quality with no fancy foreign names, and the whole contained in an old-fashioned building comfortably surrounded by as large a number of other buildings as circumstances permitted. It was worth taking time and effort to find a suitable base to work from. So he headed for Bala, since it appeared to be the largest town in his territory and therefore most likely to include such a hostelry as he had in mind.

On arrival, Bala only barely earned the Staunton seal of approval. The main street was shorter than was entirely comfortable but redeemed itself by possession of a fish and chip shop and another establishment which promised home-baked meat pies, a delicacy of which he was very fond. There were even back streets from which it was impossible to glimpse the surrounding countryside. Taken all round, Bala would probably pass muster.

After some aimless driving and a few carefully worded enquiries, Bob parked outside a public house with the unlikely name of The Yellow Fox. The building was of Victorian architecture, squashed in between two taller terraced houses in a rather dingy back street. The paintwork was chocolate brown, the stonework stained with moss and lichen and the paint on the sign above the door was peeling so badly that the once yellow fox looked more like a pair of scruffy ducklings. On the opposite side of the road was a grim-faced launderette and on the nearest corner a dusty and sombre-looking funeral parlour. It is doubtful if the local tourist board would have placed this particular street high on its list of attractions but to Bob it offered great promise.

He parked the car and entered the only bar of The Yellow Fox, noting the faded sign in the window which said 'B. and B. Food'.

It was barely opening time and the bar was empty. There was the delightful sour-sweet smell of yesterday's beer. Despite the sunshine a coal fire was burning in an open grate in one wall and one could imagine that with the door and windows closed on a cold night and the bar full, a comfortable drinking fug would be built up. The chocolate brown decor had been continued inside the building and the walls had been gloss painted in a pleasing cream, now browning off in patches where tobacco smoke took most effect, and were hung with old wooden-framed pictures whose only merit was age. The bar itself was almost certainly the original Victorian installation, a picturesque arrangement of heavy polished wood and mirrors decorated with intricate scroll designs. The room was clean but not offensively so and if the cracking paint on the ceiling and the threadbare carpet added to the general down-at-heel appearance of the establishment it also managed to promote a friendly and informal atmosphere.

Bob grunted his satisfaction and seated himself on an old wooden stool, the seat of which had been highly polished by thousands of posteriors over many years.

'Anybody home?' he yelled.

A man entered through a door set in the wall behind the bar. So enormous was his girth that he had to turn slightly sideways in order to get through. He was no taller than Bob but must have outweighed him by many stones. His completely bald head sloped down to heavy jowls, several overlapping double chins, a barrel chest and a truly magnificent stomach supported by two short legs as thick as tree trunks. He was wearing a spotlessly white shirt, a gaudily patterned V-neck pullover and a pair of grey flannel trousers, the belt of which dipped out of sight beneath his paunch. His huge face split into an amiable grin.

' 'Ullo mate,' he said. 'What's yer fancy?'

Already considerably taken aback by the man's appearance, Bob was even more surprised to hear an accent that could only have derived from near London. 'You weren't brought up on no leeks,' he said, 'you ain't no more Welsh than I am.'

'No, mate. East End. You?'

'Thereabouts.' Bob stuck out his hand and it disappeared in a mound of flesh. 'Bob Staunton.'

'Alf King. Glad ter see yer. Wot'll you 'ave?'

There followed a convivial half-hour after which Bob judged that the time had come to return to the object of his visit. 'You do rooms, that right, Alf?'

'Yeah. Just a couple.'

'Food and all?'

' 'Course.'

'I mean all meals, not just bed and breakfast?'

'The lot.'

Bob slid off the stool and prowled round the bar like a dog circling before settling to sleep. 'You ain't recommended in any of them good food guides or nothin', are you?' he asked.

Alf shook his head regretfully and his chins wobbled like jelly. ' 'Fraid not, Bob.'

'And you ain't got none of them stars, like hotels?'

'No mate. Nuffin' like that. You want that, there's plenty of places ...'

'No, mate. I don't want it. Suppose the grub's good, eh? Lookin' at you it ought to be.'

Alf King slapped his stomach and laughed heartily. The sound echoed round the room like a rumble of thunder. 'Didn't get this livin' on lettuce.' He hammered on the door behind him. ' 'Ere, Glynis, come out 'ere a minit.'

In any other company Glynis King would have seemed at least Junoesque. She had a mass of black curly hair, a round, handsome face, an expansive chest and hips that a weightlifter would have approved of but she was saved from plainness by a beautifully clear skin and dark flashing eyes. Despite her substantial figure, beside Bob Staunton and her husband she looked almost sylph-like. She smiled shyly at Bob and looked enquiringly up at her massive spouse.

'Yes, Alfred?' she enquired. Her voice was remarkably soft and gentle.

'Meet Bob Staunton . . . me missus, Glynis.'

'Nice to meet you, luv,' Bob said.

'Pleasure, I'm sure,' she replied. Her accent was definitely local.

'Bob wants ter know if you c'n cook,' Alf said bluntly.

Glynis lowered her eyes modestly. 'Never had no complaints I know of,' she said.

'You got yourselves a lodger,' said Bob, 'and I warn you, I like me grub.'

'You'll lose no weight 'ere,' Alf promised.

'Righto, Alf, I'll bring in me case.'

45

Bob was shown up to a small single room on the first floor that overlooked a yard at the rear of the building. The yard was strewn with beer barrels and crates of empty bottles. There was not a field to be seen. The bed and the furniture were old but comfortable. Bob could hardly have asked for more.

'Bathroom's second right, kharsie's next door. Meals get served in the back room next to the kitchen. You in fer lunch?' Alf enquired.

'Wouldn't miss it for the world,' Bob confirmed.

He unpacked leisurely, then found his way down to the bar and squeezed in a couple more measures of malt before lunch. The meal almost beat him. He made a point of complimenting Glynis before he struggled back up the stairs to his bedroom. Having arrived there he remembered a question he should have asked before. He returned downstairs to the bar and found Alf King closing up.

'You got a telephone, Alf?' he asked.

'Yeah, in the kitchen.'

'Mind if I use it now and then?'

'Fill yer boots, mate.'

Bob telephoned Chief Superintendent Davies and left his telephone number and address. Leo had not yet made contact. Glynis was busily at work with the washing-up and if she had any interest in his conversation she did not show it. By now the Glenfiddich and the heavy meal had taken their toll. Climbing the stairs required a considerable effort. Bob decided to lie down on the bed whilst he considered his next move.

Five minutes later he was sound asleep.

Leo was in no hurry. Unlike Bob Staunton he had no fixed ideas about the kind of accommodation he should seek and he had an acute appreciation of the lush and beautiful countryside through which he drove.

Bob Staunton's car followed him out of Betws-y-coed but then turned off and was soon out of sight. For want of a better idea he decided to drive round the outer perimeter of their alloted area and by so doing unknowingly trailed Bob into

46

the town of Bala. He stopped there to buy pre-packed food for lunch, then continued his journey, taking the A4212 out of Bala towards Trawsfynydd and Ffestiniog. Where the road ran along-side Llyn Celyn, he pulled off the road beside the lake and consulted his map. He was faintly surprised to see that by chance he had stopped quite close to the spot where the climber John Williams had been killed. It seemed a propitious moment to view the scene of the murder.

Leo drove slowly until he saw the track leading off the main road towards Moel Celyn, took it, and stopped where a series of tyre marks on the grass verge indicated the vehicles of the police investigating team had been parked. He took the map and a pair of binoculars, thoughtfully provided by Chief Superintendent Davies, and began a gentle walk up the slopes towards the moun-tain. He stopped after half a mile and by reference to the map and use of the binoculars was able to pick out the chimney which Williams had been climbing when he was shot and the knoll where the killer had lain. A sparrowhawk hovered above the knoll, then dived down to the ground to reappear seconds later and swoop away out of sight behind the rising ground. There was neither sight nor sound of human beings. The massive rock mound of Moel Celyn sat impassive in the sun, revealing nothing.

Leo returned to his car and drove on to Trawsfynydd, turned right and later passed through Ffestiniog. The road then began to climb again to Blaenau Ffestiniog, where opencast slate mining had ripped apart the encircling mountains to show their black hearts. Terraced houses huddled together near the road at the foot of the mountains amidst the towering piles of slate and rock debris as if in fear of retribution for the damage their occupants had done. Despite the sun, the whole area looked grimy and sad, as if still depressed by this ancient rape.

Opencast mining had proved the more profitable way of ex-tracting the slate since it was easier to use the machinery that could work more quickly, more effectively and more cheaply than men. But as other materials replaced slate in the con-struction industry the mines had closed and were now in the main derelict. Nature was struggling to regain what had been lost. On the tips, stunted trees and scrub rhododendrons grew and hopeful grasses found here and there a niche to cling to. There was an inescapable atmosphere of decay and regret and Leo drove quickly, anxious to be gone.

He pushed on and completed his circuit when he returned to Betws-y-coed. Here he stopped and consulted the map. There was yet ample time to find lodgings, so he elected to visit the venue of the second killing, on the Penmachno to Yspyty Ifan road, roughly in the centre of his northern half of their area of search. He took the B4406 and turned left at Penmachno, on to the lonely minor road where Nurse James had met her death. He found the spot without difficulty, parked the car and set out on a short tour of inspection. There were still marks on the road where the moped had ground along after its rider was dead, and some 400 yards away was the low, rocky mound which had hidden the killer. The road was a single strip of tarmac winding its way between low hills and on either side was short, stunted grass affording no immediate cover. The knoll stood up no more than five or six feet from the level of the road and had a fringe of rocks round the rim, similar to the hiding place the killer had found at Moel Celyn. Leo wondered if there might be any significance in that fact.

He returned to his car and drove on to Yspyty Ifan where he turned right on to a slightly improved road which led towards a particularly mountainous and evidently unpopulated area shown on the map as Migneint. It was by now early afternoon and hunger nibbled at his belly. He pulled off the road and opened up the food he had brought. He sat half in and half out of the driver's seat as he ate and contemplated the landscape.

It was similar terrain to that in the area where Nurse James had been shot. This was high table land and from the car the thick, coarse grass looked to afford easy going but when Leo, having finished his meal, walked out on to it he discovered that this was far from the case. The coarse grasses were soft and springy, sometimes a foot high, with thick moss and heather between the tufts. It was wet underfoot, this was an upland bog and there were shallow peat holes filled with brackish stagnant water. Here and there were deeper holes, covered by grasses, real ankle traps. This was no place to walk in the dark, no place for town shoes.

Leo returned to the car and sat deep in thought. As a result of his observations so far that day he had come to one firm conclusion. The killer was operating on foot. The only car tracks found at Moel Celyn when the police first arrived were those made by the dead man's vehicle. Nor were any tyre marks found at the scene of the second killing. It was true that there he could have parked on the road, but he would surely not have risked attracting attention by doing so. If he had, even on that sparsely used road, someone surely would have noticed the vehicle. In neither case had any signs been found to indicate that he had used any other form of transport, not so much as a horse's hoof had disturbed the area round where he had lain in wait. So he was operating on foot. And that confirmed Davies' theory that he was a local man. As Leo had seen for himself, this was no terrain for the uninitiated.

An old blue Landrover towing a closed trailer drove past as Leo sat in thought. It stopped a few hundred yards further on and a man got out. He went to the back of the vehicle and opened the rear door, whereupon two black and white sheepdogs leapt down and milled anxiously about as he locked the vehicle. The man set off surefootedly across the treacherous surface of the boggy grassland, heading towards the nearest hills where a straggling flock of sheep stippled the upper slopes.

Leo watched the man for a while, then started his car and drove on.

The killer had been up on Migneint most of the day. He had travelled light, taking only a packet of food, some water and a pair of binoculars. Mid-morning he had found a suitable spot from which to observe the road and had settled in to wait. Whilst he did so he studied the ground between himself and the road.

It was going to be difficult. Cover was sparse and the ground boggy and treacherous. There were other problems. This was the second day he had watched the farmer and the man clearly had no set routine. He had arrived at different times on each day. Exactly what the farmer was doing was uncertain but it seemed that for some reason he was cutting a small number of sheep out of the flock each day and taking them off in the trailer. The stalk would be particularly difficult because of the presence of the dogs and especially the near-wild sheep which he knew were as nervous as kittens and would react instantly if they got wind of him. That was fine. Without such problems it would not be a stalk but a turkey shoot and there was no pleasure in easy slaughter.

He felt for the wind and gauged the temperature in his mind, wondered if for once the weather forecast for the next day would prove reliable. A movement caught his eye. A car which had been parked whilst the single occupant ate his lunch had moved off. Undoubtedly a tourist, of no account. But he must remember to check that there was no traffic on the road at the moment he made the kill or the shot might be heard. That was another problem. He smiled distantly as he returned his attention to the farmer, and he was conscious of the thrill of anticipation.

Tomorrow he would kill. The farmer's movements were erratic. At any time he might decide he had taken enough sheep from the flock and be lost as a target. It would have to be tomorrow.

He pushed the binoculars into the breast pocket of his camouflage jacket and rolled over on to his back, staring up at the clear blue sky.

He could not remember when he had been so happy.

CHAPTER FIVE

After leaving Migneint, Leo drove on until he saw a lesser road on his right, signposted to Penmachno and Betws-y-coed, which he realized must almost bisect his half of the search area. So he took it and after a while the road began a gentle descent, which soon became a steep gradient, leading down to a long straight bordered by a forest of conifers.

As he entered the cover of the trees Leo saw a faded and rickety sign which announced 'Llety y Brecwast'. One did not have to have mastered the Welsh language to decipher that. A rather drunken arrow pointed down a dirt track that wound away between the trees. On impulse Leo turned off down the track. It was well into the afternoon and he ought now to settle the matter of lodgings.

Half a mile further on he began to doubt the honesty of the sign. The track had narrowed, become rutted and holed and the trees had closed in above him, completely blotting out the sky. Eventually he came to a fork and there was no sign to direct him. He stopped the car and got out. The single pine in front of which the track divided showed two nail holes, suggesting it had once held a sign, and eventually he found it, lying almost covered by pine needles nearby. This sign, even more badly faded than the first, simply said 'Dhys-Gla', which afforded him no assistance whatsoever. He was about to give up and return to the road when he heard the soft clip-clop of horse's hooves approaching down the righthand fork.

The horse was a well-built black gelding which must have stood sixteen hands or more and the girl in the saddle seemed almost doll-like by comparison. She was dressed in worn jodhpurs, a man's check shirt, and a dull green safari jacket, and her dark brown hair, auburn tinted, was pulled starkly back and controlled by a headscarf. Her face was broad and the features strongly formed, with a well defined chin and high cheekbones. She did not immediately strike Leo as being beautiful. Her mouth was perhaps too generous, her straight nose a little too short, her grey-green eyes obscured by unglamorous spectacles. She wore no make-up and her nose was dusted with freckles. She could have been eighteen or twenty-five, there was really no telling, except that the determined set of the chin and the confident way she sat her horse suggested she had some time ago escaped the traumatic uncertainties that normally beset the teenager.

She smiled at Leo. 'Lost, are you?' she enquired. Her voice was soft and melodic, her accent very much of North Wales, where English is only a second language.

Strangely for him, Leo found himself fumbling for words. 'Er . . . yes . . . I was . . . there was a sign . . .' he returned her smile and pointed back towards the road, '. . . the sign said "bed and breakfast". At least, I think that was what it said.'

The girl pointed down the lefthand fork. 'You'll find the house down there. It's only a short distance, on your left, you can't miss it.'

Leo nodded and smiled, got back into his car feeling rather foolish, aware that the girl was still watching him. 'Thank you,' he called, and promptly crashed the gears to add to his confusion.

He travelled a hundred yards before he regained his composure. When he looked in the rear mirror he saw that she had followed him down the track but was holding the big horse back to a walk.

The enveloping conifers suddenly gave way to giant rhododendron bushes and between them there was a view of a long wasp-waisted valley, part shadowed as the sun dropped below the encircling hills, then the track ended abruptly in a disordered farmyard littered with ancient and mostly rusty farm equipment and inhabited by a scattering of chickens and ducks. The farmhouse was stone-built and larger than Leo had expected so far from the beaten track. The windows were leaded and wisteria and mottled ivy climbed the walls and hung down over the columned porch above which, scored into the stonework, was the name 'Dhys-Gla'.

There was no sign of human life but a plume of smoke struggled up from one of the stumpy chimneys set low into the peaked slate roof. Leo got out of the car and since he could see no bell, knocked on the door. When this elicited no reply he wandered round the side of the house, from which direction he could hear the occasional dull thunk of an axe on wood. He found himself in a complex of outhouses, some overflowing with hay, one housing an elderly tractor, two more which served as stables, a third which seemed to be full of empty apple boxes and others whose functions were unclear. There were more chickens and ducks and behind the outbuildings Leo could see a small paddock in which were a small grey mare and a rather irritable-looking goat tethered by a chain. Beyond the paddock was a pond encircled with yew and alder trees.

Leo finally located the wielder of the axe in one of the further outhouses. He was a man of sixty or more, short and stocky, with a fine head of crinkly grey hair. His face and arms were tanned deep brown and from the way he hefted the long-handled axe he was still very fit. Although he was roughly dressed, his clothes old and worn, he had the face and bearing of a patrician and there was about him an aura of firm confidence.

He looked up when Leo's shadow fell across him. 'Ah, looking for me, are you?' His voice was deep and resonant, the voice of a younger man.

'I did try the house,' Leo said, 'but there was no reply.'

'All out, they are. Never mind. You'll be wanting bed and breakfast?'

'And an evening meal, if possible.'

'No doubt we can manage that. Daffyd Johns,' he added, pushing out his hand.

Leo took it. The grip was firm but not arrogantly hard.

'Leo Wyndsor,' Leo replied.

'Come up to the house, boy. I'll show you the rooms. There's no one else staying at present, so you have a choice. Tell the truth, we don't get many visitors, out of the way here, see?'

Johns led the way back to the house. For want of conversation Leo said: 'The sign on the main road has seen better days, I very nearly missed it. No doubt you would do better trade if it had a touch of paint and was perhaps resited.'

'Oh, we're not so worried you know,' Johns said diffidently, 'we do well enough, the Lord provides and greed doesn't become a man, does it now?'

'Indeed not,' Leo agreed, feeling he had been politely but firmly put in his place.

'On holiday are you, Leo?' Johns asked with easy familiarity.

'No, I'm not actually. I'm a freelance reporter,' Leo lied.

'Ah, them shootings ... bad business that, bad business. You'll be staying a while, then?'

'I'm not sure. Probably several weeks. Rather depends on how things go.'

The house smelt of elderly furniture, country cooking and log fires. It was clean and tidy but had an overall air of genteel decay. The carpets, curtains and furniture were all of good quality but were showing their age. Yet they fitted the house, having grown old with it and not without some grace. The ceilings were wood-beamed, the floors on ground level stone-flagged, giving the house a feeling of permanence. Somewhere an old clock ticked heavy and slow. So far as Leo could see, no compromise had been made for the benefit of visitors; this was a home not a pseudo hotel, one took it as it was or not at all.

Leo selected a bedroom at the rear, overlooking the valley, and settled the modest price with Daffyd Johns who seemed vaguely embarrassed even to talk of money.

'Is there a telephone?' Leo asked. 'I should need to use it

quite often I'm afraid but by all means make a generous allowance for that on the bill.'

'In the hall,' Johns said. 'You're welcome. You'll be ringing to London, no doubt?'

'Yes. And to our office in Portmadoc and sometimes to a colleague of mine who is also in this area working on the same story. Will I be able to have a meal tonight?'

'Oh yes. But . . . if you don't mind, since you're on your own, we'll all eat together?'

'By all means,' Leo said, not being anxious to dine in lone splendour.

Despite Leo's protestations, Daffyd Johns insisted on bringing in his case and then making a cup of tea for them both, which they took in the huge old-fashioned kitchen. As they talked, Leo discovered that Johns, now retired, had been an Anglican priest and still occasionally preached locally. He eked out his small pension by subsistance farming on his five acres and occasional summer letting. He was a comfortable man to talk to, open and uncomplicated, intelligent and above all, content.

After they had been talking for a while the girl walked into the kitchen. Leo stood awkwardly as she entered. She crossed to Daffyd Johns and kissed him lightly on the forehead. She had removed her headscarf and her hair, rather more auburn than Leo remembered, cascaded about her shoulders. She was taller than she had seemed on the horse, with a slim but well rounded figure. She took off her glasses and thrust them self-consciously into the pocket of her safari jacket and Leo found himself staring into her grey-green eyes longer than good manners allowed.

'Meet Leo Wyndsor, he'll be staying with us a while,' Johns said to the girl, then, to Leo, 'my daughter, Nerys.'

'We met, actually' Leo said, smiling at her, 'but you did not say you were the daughter of the house.' He held out his hand and she took it across the table.

'There was no need,' she said, 'I knew I'd be seeing you again soon enough.' She turned to her father. 'You men may have nothing to do but I have. Morwenna and young Jones will be back soon and if you want to eat tonight I'll need the kitchen to myself . . . are you eating with us, Leo?'

'If it is convenient.'

'Of course. Now, if you don't mind . . .' She ushered the two men firmly out through the door and closed it behind them.

'Take a tip from an old man, my son,' Johns said. 'Never interfere in the kitchen . . . every woman should have her kingdom. We eat at seven, I'll see you then.' And he disappeared back into the farmyard.

Leo went to his room, unpacked, took a bath and changed out of his suit into more casual attire. Having yet half an hour to wait for the meal, he lay on the bed and turned his mind to the murder enquiry. At least, he tried to, but found his thoughts returning again and again to Nerys Johns. She seemed to have had the oddest effect on him. He could never recall a time when he did not have a facility with words and he was always completely at ease in the company of women. It was doubtful if he could now remember the names of all those he had taken to his bed or who had taken him to theirs. Yet in the company of Nerys Johns he had been gauche and awkward, like an inexperienced teenager. It rankled, offended his ego.

In his mind, he recalled every word that had passed between them in their two brief meetings, looking for meanings he might have missed. Had she been laughing at him? Once he thought he had caught a look in her eye, as though she knew he was off balance with her. It made no sense. Had she been stunningly beautiful he could perhaps have understood it, but she was not. She did not attract him in the slightest, no, not at all. So why should he concern himself about what she thought of him? He wondered why she wore those ugly glasses when she could have had contact lenses. Perhaps later, when he knew her better, he would ask her. She must have thought him a damn fool, hesitating and struggling over the most banal of conversations.

Daffyd Johns was calling to him up the stairs. Half an hour had flown by. He went down to the kitchen where the long refectory table had been laid for the meal and was introduced to Morwenna and young Jones. Morwenna was a spinster of Daffyd

56

Johns' age, distantly related to him, a second cousin or similar, a small hunched woman with sharp features and intelligent eyes deep set in a thin face. The other resident, young Jones, was so named to distinguish him from his father, old Jones, approaching his century and still hale and hearty, but young Jones had certainly seen seventy years himself.

Daffyd Johns sat at the head of the table with Nerys and Leo on one side and Morwenna and young Jones on the other. Johns said a prayer of thanks before the meal. Leo, to whom public prayer would normally have been an embarrassment, closed his eyes and dropped his head, accepting this as a normal ritual in the household, and was faintly surprised that he did not find the moment personally trying.

The meal was excellent but afterwards Leo could not have recalled what they ate. The conversation flowed easily and Leo in no way felt excluded from this intimate circle. It was as if, on the instant and without enquiry, they had accepted him as one of them. Only with Morwenna and young Jones did Leo experience some mild difficulty since their command of English was hardly complete and their heavy accent made it difficult to follow their conversation. Occasionally one or other of them lapsed into Welsh, though quickly reverting to English with an apology to their guest.

Later they all went into the sitting-room where a log fire burned in the open grate and an old upright piano took the place of the television that would have been found in other households. Daffyd Johns produced a bottle of home-made blackberry wine and poured it generously. After a tentative sip, Leo rapidly came to the conclusion that half a bottle would probably be lethal.

Nerys played the piano, the others sang, Leo hummed the tunes and time drifted by unnoticed. There was a sense of communal warmth, of a family united and certain of itself, of an almost tribal, but not exclusive, cultural self-sufficiency. Leo was borne along on a tide of friendliness and undemanding acceptance and he was vaguely disappointed when Daffyd indicated he intended to retire for the night.

Leo was in his bedroom when he suddenly remembered that

he had not informed anyone of his whereabouts. He went back down to the hall, dialled the number of the incident room at Portmadoc, gave his address and telephone number and was told Bob Staunton had already enquired twice about him. Anticipating some of Bob's earthier language, Leo telephoned the number he was given.

'Where the bloody hell've you been?' Bob enquired.

'I've had a busy day,' Leo replied, 'but I've settled myself in now. Would you like to make a note of the address?'

'Yeah. Hang on . . . right, fire away.'

Leo provided the details and promised faithfully to ring again the next day. It was apparent from his speech that Bob had found a hostelry that was to his liking and had been hard at the Glenfiddich, so Leo did not prolong the conversation.

As he passed the kitchen door on his way up the stairs, Leo could hear the voices of Morwenna and Nerys chattering away in Welsh. He would have liked to have joined them for a while, perhaps even have offered his help, but somehow the fact that they were not speaking English deterred him.

He returned to his bedroom, undressed and got into bed taking with him a clipboard and pen. He began to make notes of his thoughts on the case so far. But within minutes the clipboard had fallen from his hands and he was fast asleep.

Bob Staunton, normally an early riser, woke late the following morning to the sound of traffic in the street outside The Yellow Fox. His throat felt dry and his head ached. In the bar the previous evening Bob had learned first hand of the Welsh zeal for hospitality. There was a cup of tea on the small table beside his bed but it was cold. Evidently Glynis had decided to let him sleep on.

He grunted in annoyance. He was used to taking his drink and still getting up with the lark. A wash and shave and two aspirins later, however, he felt much recovered and was able to do justice to a considerable breakfast before leaving his temporary home.

He was determined, having wasted the previous afternoon and spent the evening in convivial company but to no good effect, that today he would redeem himself by his industry. His intention was to visit the scenes of the two murders, then familiarize himself with the area of search, much as Leo had done, before settling down to a systematic infiltration of the local population.

Bob drove round the perimeter of the search area as far as Pentrefoelas, then cut off to visit the scene of the killing of the nurse on the Penmachno to Yspyty Ifan road before returning to the main road and continuing his circuit. He passed through Blaenau Ffestiniog, where the ugly scars of the opencast mining did not offend him anywhere near as much as they had Leo, then through Ffestiniog and eventually turned left at Trawsfynydd on the return road to Bala. At a bend in the road approaching Llyn Celyn, close to the spot where the climber had been killed, he was overtaken by a powerful motor-cycle which promptly cut in on him, forcing him to brake and pull over. By the time he had regained control of the car and passed Anglo-Saxon comment on the parentage of the motor-cyclist, the offending vehicle had disappeared ahead.

It being now well past opening time, Bob drove straight on into Bala intending to lunch at The Yellow Fox and complete his circuit with a visit to the scene of the murder at Moel Celyn in the afternoon. In the town he was forced to stop behind a line of vehicles held up by an articulated lorry that was sprawled across the road, attempting to reverse into a narrow service alley. One car in front of him was the offending motor-cyclist revving his machine impatiently as he waited for the road to clear.

All Bob could see of the rider was a broad leather-clad back with the word 'Ace' stamped out across it in metal studs. The rider's head was enclosed in a black helmet with face visor and he wore black leather trousers and knee-length jackboots. A Nazi swastika was stencilled on to the back of the helmet and a set of bright metal spurs was buckled on to the rider's jackboots.

Bob's lips tightened. He was an unashamed reactionary when it came to the wilder elements of youthful society, to whom he applied the generic term 'the great unwashed', and for the leather brigade he had an especial distaste. It was beyond his comprehension why even the most insensitive yobbo should want to imitate the very evil his generation had fought to destroy. His dislike of the jackboot and the leather uniform even extended to the unfortunate members of the police traffic patrols who had no control over the uniform issued to them, but whom he often slightingly referred to as 'the gestapo'. So Bob viewed the young man who had cut him up on the bend near Moel Celyn a few minutes before with an interest that was not entirely altruistic. Given the opportunity he intended to pass on a few home truths.

That opportunity did not, however, occur. Before Bob could get out of his car the driver of the articulated lorry finally managed to insert the rear end of the vehicle into the tiny service alley and clear the road. The motor-cyclist took off with a snarl of noise and turned into a minor road that led out of Bala itself towards Bala Lake.

By the time Bob had regained the sanity and comfort of the bar of The Yellow Fox, he had almost forgotten the incident.

'Do any good?' Alf King asked.

'Eh?'

'D'you get a story for the paper or anythin'?'

'Oh ... no, not really,' Bob said, annoyed with himself at having quite forgotten the lie about his occupation he had told the night before.

'S 'pose they still pay you like, if you don't get a story?'

'How'd I live, else?'

'Yeah, but I thought, you being freelance like you said, maybe you only got paid when you got a story, with me?'

Bob did not find it easy to live a lie. Alf King had caught him out without even trying.

'A job like this, someone'll always pick up me expenses,' he said. 'Now, do I get a snifter or've you joined the Temperance League?'

Alf grinned, levered his vast bulk round, poured Bob a measure from the Glenfiddich bottle and allowed himself a half of bitter.

'That's on me, mate,' he said. 'Should mind me own business.'

'Your astonishin' good health,' Bob said. 'What's for dinner?'

'Bit of beef, mate. Nice bit of beef.'

'You come into money, Alf?'

'Nah. Local farmer, got 'is own slaughter 'ouse. 'Ee scratches my back, I scratch 'is, know what I mean?' Alf winked heavily and his left eye disappeared in a roll of fat.

'May he prosper,' said Bob, downing his drink.

Over lunch he put his mind to the job in hand. It occurred to him to wonder if, despite what Davies had said, the killer had any previous convictions. Since they had no idea of his identity the thought did not take him very far, but it seemed worth checking to see what other crimes of violence had taken place in the area recently where guns had been used. The shootings had both taken place on a weekday, during normal working hours, which suggested that either the killer was on holiday from his employment, or that he was not employed on a normal weekly basis, or that he was not employed at all. But he had to get money from somewhere and violent crime seemed to Bob to be a logical alternative.

Having finished his meal he wandered into the kitchen and found Glynis King washing-up.

'I've got news for you, me luv,' he said. 'You *can* cook.'

'Thank you kindly, Bob,' Glynis said, smiling coyly at him. 'Had enough, did you?'

'I'm fit to bust,' Bob said. 'Listen, I've got to make a phone call, private like, d'you mind?'

'Only too glad to leave the washing up,' Glynis said.

'Won't take a minute, sorry and all that.'

'Don't fuss about it, make your call, I'll go upstairs and finish here later.'

When Glynis had left the room Bob dialled the incident room number and was put through to Sergeant Richards.

'That you, Gwyn?'

'Yes, sir.'

'Listen, mate. Since you're sittin' about scratching your rear end, why don't you run a check on all crimes this year where the villains used guns?'

'We did that, sir. Not one case in the last five years of a rifle being used in a crime.'

'Not rifles, mate, *anythin*'. He could have a bloody arsenal for all we know.'

'Okay, sir. Just this area?'

'No. The whole of Wales. He might not be that local, might he? If you come up with anythin', check the spent bullets or cases against what we got on our job, right?'

'Will be done, sir.'

'See you, son.'

Bob replaced the receiver, stuck his head out into the hall and yelled up the stairs. 'Kitchen's free, Glynis.'

'Thank you, Bob,' Glynis answered distantly.

'I'll be back for tea,' Bob yelled.

'Cold beef do yer?' Alf's voice enquired.

'Not half,' Bob replied. 'See you later.'

Unlike Bob Staunton, Leo had woken that morning feeling rested, relaxed and eager to face the day. This was an unusual circumstance. He was usually far from his best until long after the sun was up.

He took breakfast in the farm kitchen, attended by Morwenna and Nerys, Daffyd and young Jones having long since started their day's work.

'Will you be back for lunch, Leo?' Nerys asked, as he stood to leave the room.

'I'm not sure. I shall find a quiet spot where I can sit and think.'

'Don't you have a story to write . . . or whatever you do?'

She was wearing faded old jeans and a loose sweater. Leo would have been quite content to spend the morning in the kitchen, chatting idly with her, watching her work. He felt no inclination to work himself. In this house nothing was apparently done with any sense of urgency and something of the slower pace of life here seemed to have affected him.

'I have nothing to write as yet,' he said.

'You could use the front room if you wished.'

'I'd rather be outside.'

'Then there's an old log in the paddock . . . I sit there myself sometimes when I want to be alone. You'll not be disturbed.'

Leo collected his clipboard and wandered across the farmyard, through the outbuildings and down to the paddock. The sky
was again clear and the sun surprisingly warm for September.
There was a profusion of birds in the surrounding conifers and
bees still droned about their business amongst the dandelions in
the paddock, ignoring the human intruder.

'Don't talk to Bouncer,' Nerys had said. 'He can be a dreadful
grump with strangers.' But the goat seemed securely tethered
and contented itself with glaring balefully at Leo as he took his
seat. The only other occupants of the paddock were Merry, the
grey mare, and Red, the inappropriately named black gelding
that Nerys had been riding the previous day.

The view from the paddock was restricted by the encircling
conifers which overhung the drystone walls, a solid phalanx of
dark green guarding the oasis of grass. Leo had intended to work,
he really had, but in the end he dreamed the morning away. And
every moment he was aware of the girl who was not beautiful,
who did not attract him, who was preparing food in the kitchen,
or perhaps cleaning the house or making beds or talking to Morwenna or singing to herself or . . .

She came down to fetch him for lunch, sat for a moment on the
log beside him. His clipboard lay discarded on the grass in front
of them.

'Did you get your thinking done?' Nerys asked.

She was sitting a foot away from him, they were not looking at
each other, yet he was vividly aware of her.

No,' Leo said. 'I ate of the lotus.'

Nerys laughed. 'A land in which it seemed always afternoon,'
she quoted. 'Others have said the same. There is something here
that affects people that way.'

'Something or someone,' Leo said.

'Do you ride?' Nerys asked. It was as if she had not heard him.
'A little.'

'We could ride up to the head of the valley this afternoon . . .
if you were not too busy, that is?'

There was a battered old Landrover in the farmyard when

they returned to the house. The unexpected guest was ex-Major Thomas, a family friend and near neighbour, a man in his late sixties, still straight backed, lean and brown with vivid blue eyes. Daffyd Johns introduced Leo and over lunch the conversation was general. Not until the older men had lit their pipes did Major Thomas make the remark that jerked Leo out of his reverie and back into the harsh world of death and duty.

'The police still haven't caught that chap, then,' he said.

Daffyd looked at Leo. 'Unless you know more than the papers tell?' he said.

Leo shook his head. 'I'm afraid not.'

'Mad he may be . . . but if what you newspaper fellows say is half true he must be a fantastic shot,' Thomas continued.

'Tommy knows,' Daffyd confided to Leo. 'Shot at Bisley, he has.'

'Really?' Leo looked at the Major with new interest.

The Major sucked at his pipe and looked modestly up at the ceiling. 'Once or twice,' he said.

'Went right through the last war,' Daffyd added.

'Do you still shoot?' Leo asked.

'Not really. Potter about with the old shotgun, you know. Oh, I've still got the match rifle, still keep my licence up but it's been many a year since I shot in competition.'

'What do you make of this chap, then?'

'This killer of yours? Mad as a hatter no doubt . . . but in the war I'd have given my right arm for a few snipers like him.'

Sniper. The single word reverberated round Leo's brain like an alarm bell. For the first time since he arrived at Dhys-Gla his mind was entirely on his work. 'Major, I'd like to talk to you again about this . . . may I come to see you sometime?'

'Certainly. Be glad of the company. Daffyd'll tell you where to find me.'

Leo excused himself, went into the hall and telephoned the incident office at Portmadoc. Eventually Chief Superintendent Davies came to the telephone.

'Yes, Leo. Found him, have you?' Davies joked.

'Not quite yet, sir, but something has just occurred to me and I wanted to ask you about it.'

'Fire away.'

'Perhaps I have the wrong end of the stick, but when we were talking about our man we all seemed to be assuming that he had acquired his expertise with a rifle in competition shooting ... I certainly did.'

'So did we all.'

'It occurs to me that he might have been army trained.'

Davies laughed. Leo could imagine his generous double chin wobbling. 'The average infantryman couldn't hit a barn door at ten paces.'

'I had in mind a trained sniper,' Leo said.

There was silence for a moment. Then Davies said: 'Taking his holidays doing a little practice killing in Snowdonia, you think?' There was just the faintest tinge of sarcasm evident. Davies was not quite sure of his ground.

'Not exactly. I wasn't actually thinking of a serving soldier, although nothing is impossible. I had in mind the fact that we are agreed that he is a psychopath. Just possibly the army discovered what he was like and declined his further services.'

'And he's trying to prove something?'

'Perhaps.'

'Well now, that's a thought.'

'I imagine we'll have to channel our enquiry through the Home Office. The army keeps its snipers under wraps and they may not care to publicize their failures,' Leo suggested.

'They weren't very forthcoming when we enquired about the rifle and ammunition. Leave it to me. I'll let you know,' Davies promised.

'If it involves meeting someone ... I'd like to go.'

Whilst Leo was talking on the telephone, Daffyd saw his old friend to his Landrover.

'What's ailing Nerys?' the Major asked.

'Oh, nothing's ailing her, Tommy,' Daffyd said, grinning.

Major Thomas smiled. 'What d'you know of the young man?' he asked.

'Not a lot. But more than Nerys does.'

'Good-looking boy.'

'Yes. Been staggering about like a lopped chicken ever since he set eyes on Nerys.'

'Pity he's not telling the truth,' Thomas said.

Daffyd knocked out his pipe on the heel of his boot. 'It is,' he said. 'I think, in all the circumstances, I might volunteer to clean his room this afternoon while he's out.'

'You'll let me know?'

Daffyd nodded.

'And you'll tell Nerys?'

'Yes. She's a right to know.'

Nerys came out of the kitchen as Leo replaced the receiver. 'Are you busy, can you not come riding?' she asked.

'Certainly I can come. The afternoon is ours.'

They rode down the track that led to the main road until they came to the fork where they had first met, then took the path that wound upwards through the trees, reaching for the lower slopes of the mountain at the head of the valley. The conifers began to thin, shrank to Christmas-tree size, and they were riding with the sky as a ceiling once more. They exchanged laughter and deliberately casual chatter, absorbed in the moment, leaving the horses to find their own way for much of the time.

The path finally petered out beside a ruined stone tower occupying a low grassy knoll, its blank eyes peering evermore across the valley. Leo turned to look back but Nerys stopped him. 'Wait until we get to the top. Don't look until we get to the top,' she urged.

Leo obeyed, following her lead as she picked out a path upwards between the rock outcroppings. He was suddenly conscious of a strange sensation in his stomach. He thought it was hunger, yet he knew he was not hungry, he could not have faced food. Already he had forgotten the telephone call he had made, had lost all thoughts of his work without being aware of it. She was calling to him, pointing out a spot where water was weeping down a rock face into a shallow pool surrounded by tiny, five-starred, green-bright bog plants.

A further ten minutes of steady climbing brought them to a grassed shelf at the highest point of that end of the valley.

Nerys turned her horse and waited for Leo to join her. 'You can look now,' she said.

Leo took his eyes from her for a while. Behind them, and on both sides, the mountains were folded in upon each other, sharing high green-black valleys, and with the sunlight on them the mountains looked benign, innocent, casually inviting, solidly beautiful. Ahead, falling away from the shelf on which they stood, was the steep rock-speckled hillside, then the first trees, the formal ranks of the conifers, the roofs of Dhys-Gla glimpsed beyond, then lush green fields bordered by drystone walls and here and there scattered dull-grey outbuildings. The river meandered along the valley floor, its veins collecting water from the surrounding slopes, delivering itself finally into a distant lake which was dwarfed and narrowed by perspective. And the colours were the variegated greens and the dull reds and the warm russets of autumn, merging and melting one into another in a perfect symmetry. The valley lay before them like a naked woman, earthily vital, inviting, revealing all her delights without deceit or false modesty, displaying openly the lush womb of fertility, solidly encompassed, warmly enclosed and with a gentle softness within. Here, for those who could see, were revealed the fibres of passion, beauty and primordial spirituality that tie the children of the Welsh mother so firmly to her apron strings.

This brazen display of natural voluptuousness left Leo admiring but hesitant, like a modest guest who has inadvertently discovered his beautiful hostess naked in her bath. Nerys dismounted and went to sit on a rounded, moss-capped boulder at the edge of the grassy shelf and after a moment Leo joined her.

'Don't you think it's beautiful?' Nerys asked.

Leo looked at her. 'Very beautiful,' he said.

'Daddy preached a sermon once, he referred to Wales as "the virgin harlot". It upset some of the congregation.'

'I can imagine. But I know exactly what he meant.'

'Yes, I knew you would.'

'How did you know?'

'Because we have an empathy, don't we?'

'Yes. Nerys . . .'

She cut him short. 'Look, Leo, do look!' She was pointing down the slope to where a sudden cloud of small birds, mixed chaffinches and greenfinches, had arrived at a clump of stunted gorse to conduct an excited squabble. One perched on a small rock and, unthinking, turned its back on the breeze and was paid in ruffled feathers, revealing pale cream and metallic blue underclothes. The finch, perhaps aware that it was observed, turned quickly about as if in shame, like some coy spinster.

Nerys and Leo shared a laugh and the birds flew off, squabbling still, gliding in casual formation down to the trees below.

'I come here,' Nerys said, 'if I'm sad or depressed.'

'I find it difficult to imagine you ever being sad or depressed, you seem so lively and capable.'

'Do I really? How strange. Nevertheless, sometimes I used to feel burdened by the world. After all, it's been a long wait.'

'A long wait for what?' Leo asked.

But Nerys did not answer. She took off her glasses with that sudden annoyed movement he had seen before and stuffed them into the pocket of her safari jacket.

'You don't have to take your glasses off,' Leo said, 'they make no difference.'

'They make a difference to me,' she said shortly.

'Why?'

'Because.'

'Because what?'

'Because four isn't five.'

'I don't understand . . . are you angry with me for some reason?'

Nerys stood up. 'No. But it's time to go now. I have work to do at home.'

'Nerys . . .'

But she was walking determinedly back to her horse and he was obliged to follow her. During the ride back she regained her normal even temper but still she held herself at a distance. She

68

was friendly and clearly glad to be with him, yet her attitude denied even the most innocent intimacy.

When they arrived at the farmyard Daffyd Johns was waiting for them. He took the reins of Leo's horse and offered a huge welcoming smile. Leo dismounted a little clumsily and was faintly puzzled at the older man's evident pleasure at his return.

'Enjoy your ride, my son?'

'Yes, thank you, Mr Johns.'

'Oh . . . come now, call me Daffyd.'

'Thank you, Daffyd. I will.'

'Run on then. I'll see to Red here.' He patted the horse's neck affectionately and favoured Leo with another huge smile.

At the door of the farmhouse Leo turned to look back. Nerys and Daffyd were talking intently, heads close together. Suddenly Nerys flung her arms round her father's neck and hugged him.

Leo entered the house. The girl was beyond his comprehension.

The killer had been up on Migneint since first light. He had chosen a spot on the upper slopes of the high ground, in a jumble of naked rocks that erupted like boils on the body of the mountain. He had a view of the road, a metal scar on the high plain, marked by starkly rigid telegraph poles that leant forward into the slope or leant back from it as the road rose and fell with the contours of the land. There had been little traffic to observe.

Nearer at hand the black-faced sheep cropped a slight living from the coarse grasses, spreading out along the lower slopes in haphazard formation. By mid-afternoon the sheep had worked their way along the slopes to his left and the wind had changed direction, so he moved his position to ensure that he was downwind of the flock, anxious not to disturb them. He found a semi-secure hiding place where, beside a rock, a hopeful ash tree had grown to half man-height, gnarled and twisted with the effort of survival, bent over with the weight of the wind.

Another man might have given up the hunt but the killer had patience. Now and then there were visitors in the sky, a lone gull, divorced from the sea, planing across the invisible columns of

69

rising air, or a predatory sparrowhawk pausing here and there to hover over a likely spot. The killer felt at one with the sparse wildlife of the mountains, and especially with the hawk. He killed as the hawk killed, with professional skill and without remorse.

The Landrover with the attached trailer appeared late in the afternoon and parked beside the road in exactly the same spot as it had on previous days. The farmer released his sheepdogs, locked the vehicle and set off across the scrubby grass towards the flock, the black and white dogs fanned out ahead of him, animal extensions of his being.

The killer loaded his rifle with a single round and began the stalk as soon as the farmer left the road, swinging round behind him in a wide arc, moving nearer all the time to his target, progressing in short crouched runs and by longer spells of crawling with stomach close to the ground, propelled by elbows and knees, holding the rifle carefully clear of the ground in front of him. His camouflaged clothing and woollen helmet and his dirt-streaked face rendered him invisible even at close range when he was stationary. Only when he moved would he have been seen by a trained observer and then only if his position on the lower slopes was known. The farmer was side-on to him, intent on his task.

When he had closed to within 400 yards the killer received a sudden shock. He came upon a fat-bellied ewe sat in the lee of a rock, feet tucked beneath herself, chewing the cud. She started up indignantly at his intrusion upon her privacy and set off at a run to rejoin the flock, bleating news of his whereabouts. The killer froze as the farmer turned towards him and whistled up a dog to bring the ewe in.

The dog, wolfish heritage controlled, herded the ewe towards the flock with short sharp runs, aiming her unerringly to safety at the farmer's whistle. The killer waited a full minute before moving forward again.

At a distance of 200 yards, he stopped, adjusted his body comfortably in the prone position, wrapped the padded sling tightly round his left arm and brought the rifle up to sight on his target. The dogs were cutting out individual sheep from the flock and the farmer had his back to the killer.

The distance was modest but there were factors which made the shot less than easy. The farmer was dressed in dull brown and green and, being below the skyline, he did not make a clearly defined target. There was a slightly variable wind from left to right, the sky was overcast, and the light was poor so late in the afternoon. The killer considered these factors and adjusted the scopesight to compensate.

When he was satisfied he took a last look to his right, across the road, to ensure that it was free of traffic before making the kill, then mentally prepared himself for the moment of total concentration and relaxation before he squeezed the trigger. He was not a big man, not tall or powerfully built, but he had that reserve of strength necessary to handle the heavy rifle easily without straining or tensing his muscles.

The bullet struck the burly figure of the farmer to the left of his spine below his shoulder-blade and threw him violently forward on to his face amongst the short spiky grass. The killer watched through the scopesight but the farmer lay still, the wind ruffling his thick hair, his blunt fingers motionless.

The dogs had been thrown into confusion by the whipcrack of the shot, the sheep had scattered at a run. After a while, lacking orders, the dogs returned to the body of their master, sniffing and licking at his hands and face, whining anxiously, pushing at him with their noses.

Then one of them abandoned the body and loped off down the road where, in the gathering gloom, it sat beside the empty Landrover and scratched urgently at the closed passenger door.

Up in the distant foothills the killer, who had not taken food or water all day, sheltered behind a bow-shaped rock and ate the meagre rations he had allowed himself, sharing crumbs with the sparrows who had appeared from nowhere.

CHAPTER SIX

Whilst the evening meal was being prepared in the farmhouse Leo repaired to his bedroom and sat on the edge of his bed, completing the boring but unavoidable chore of making up his official diary, in which he had to account for every minute of his working day and every penny of expenditure. It was now and then necessary to take some artistic licence since an entry reading, 'went riding with young lady', or 'sat in paddock thinking for three hours', was not guaranteed to favourably impress his senior officers. On the other hand, 'to operational area re information', or 'engaged at Dhys-Gla re collation of material', whilst less accurate, was also less likely to rouse adverse comment.

He was called down to the kitchen before he had completed the task and took his seat at the table with the family. Daffyd said grace and they all descended on the meal with gusto. Everyone seemed in high good spirits and Nerys, sitting next to Leo, particularly so, though neither of them seemed able to do justice to the excellent food. Leo was conscious of a change in the attitude of all of them towards him, especially Nerys, who took his hand under the table and held it, as if in confirmation of some previous intimacy. But if there had been such previous intimacy, Leo had missed it.

In some strange way he felt a guest no longer, but one of them. If they dropped suddenly into Welsh in the middle of the conversation they no longer stopped ånd apologized but somehow expected him to understand and they chatted in front of him of friends and family matters as if he were related to them. Leo was flattered but puzzled and made a mental note to ask Nerys about this sudden change in his status amongst them.

When the meal was over they all adjourned to the sitting-room. Daffyd produced the home-made blackberry wine and they sat around the piano whilst Nerys played. It was warm, comfortable, companionable, a world away from the normality of a detective's life. When the telephone rang, Morwenna went to answer it.

'It's for you, Leo,' she said when she returned. 'Says his name is Bob, a friend of yours, he says.'

Leo noticed Nerys and her father exchange a smile as he left the room. They were up to something, those two.

'That your bit of crumpet I was just talkin' to?' Bob asked.

'That was Morwenna. She's sixty if she's a day.'

'Wouldn't put it past you. You want the bad news first?'

'If that's all there is.'

'That's all. Our man's been at it again.'

Leo sighed. 'It had to come, I suppose.'

'Farmer out sortin' his sheep. Place called Migneint, miles from anywhere, right in the middle of my half. Single shot through the heart from about 200 yards. They only found him an hour ago.'

'No trace of the killer?'

'Not that they've found. Listen, you got your map handy?'

'No, but if you give me the map reference I'll mark it down later.'

Bob read the reference off and Leo scribbled it on a pad beside the telephone. 'Is there any point in us going there?' he asked.

'Not that I can see. What's there Davies and his boys'll find. Look, I reckon we'd better have a meet tomorrow.'

'By all means.'

'Right. Drive down to Bala, then take the Llangollen Road. Stop in the first layby on the left . . . say nine?'

'Yes. I'll be there. Do I detect that you have a lead?'

'Leo, you couldn't detect a pint of beer in a brewery. Wish I had. You?'

'I'm afraid not.'

'Ah well, early days. See you in the mornin'.'

Nerys had stopped playing when Leo left the room and when he re-entered they all looked at him expectantly.

'Everything all right, is it?' Daffyd asked.

'I'm afraid not. There's been another shooting, a sheep farmer. It happened up on Migneint, late this afternoon some time.'

'What was his name, Leo? It must be someone we know,' Nerys said, anxiously.

'I'm afraid I don't know yet. They only found the body about an hour ago.'

'Must be Dai Morgan,' young Jones said, 'do I ask Meg?'

Daffyd stood. 'No. That's my job. I was their priest for years enough.'

He went out into the hall to telephone the Morgan farm, leaving a sad silence behind him. Nerys came to sit beside Leo. 'If it *is* Dai,' she told him, 'he's father's second cousin.'

'I'm sorry, I had no idea.'

'No reason you should know. Will it be the same man that shot Gwyneth James and that climber?'

'It seems very likely.'

'When this man is caught, you won't have to be there, will you?'

'It would be a great scoop if I was but I doubt if I will be.'

The answer did not seem to reassure Nerys. Daffyd came back into the room looking grave. 'It was Dai,' he said. 'I must go over to see Meg, she's taking it badly.'

'Daffyd, don't go alone,' Leo said. 'This house is in the centre of the shootings. It's not safe for any of you to be out alone away from the house. Promise me none of you will go anywhere alone until this man is caught.'

Daffyd nodded. 'You're right Leo, and I must set an example. I'll take young Jones.'

74

'But *you* go out alone,' Nerys protested.

'I *have* to, Nerys, it's my job,' Leo answered.

'Why can't your friend Bob stay here, then you could go out with him.'

'I'm afraid that's not possible . . . and whilst I think of it, no riding by yourself, promise?'

'No! If you can risk your life for no reason, so can I!'

Daffyd intervened. 'You'll do as Leo says, Nerys. You know it makes sense.'

'If it does, then Leo should have someone with him as well.'

'You must promise,' Daffyd said sternly.

'Very well,' Nerys said stiffly, 'I promise!' She walked out of the room without saying another word.

'I do apologize . . .' Leo began.

Daffyd cut him short with a gesture. 'She's naturally upset. But you will take care of yourself, my son, won't you?'

'Only the good die young,' Leo said, attempting to lighten the moment.

'That's exactly what Nerys is afraid of,' Daffyd replied.

A few minutes before 9 a.m. the following morning Leo pulled into the layby just outside the town of Bala. At exactly the appointed time Bob Staunton drove in, parked behind him and came to sit in the front passenger seat of Leo's car.

'Hullo, mate. How's things?' he asked.

'Fine. You obviously found suitable digs.'

'So I did. Good publican, honest bloke, knows how to run a pub does Alf.'

'Meaning he stocks Glenfiddich and dispenses it on a twenty-four-hour basis.'

'Don't be bloody cheeky. You all right at this farm, look after you, do they?'

'Very well indeed.'

'Oh, yes! Hot and cold running chambermaids, eh?'

'Not a chambermaid in sight. Just charming people.'

'Daughter of the house, is there?' asked Bob slyly.

'There is . . .'

'You blushed, Leo . . .'

'I did not!'

'You bloody did, I saw you! Crumpet, is she?'

'No. I mean . . . there *is* a daughter of the house but she is not "crumpet" as you so bluntly put it, she is . . .'

'. . . charmin', you said.'

'. . . yes, but not my type, definitely not my type.'

'Meaning she don't put it about?'

'I doubt it . . . but I really wouldn't know. I'm not interested.'

'Know what I think? I think you finally met your match, my old darlin'. I reckon this one's got you by the short and curlies!' Bob chortled in evident satisfaction.

'Can we change the subject?' Leo asked primly. 'We *did* arrange this meeting for an exchange of information, as I understood it.'

Bob grinned wolfishly, delighted at having caught the usually urbane Leo Wyndsor on one foot, but he decided to let him off the hook. 'All right, mate. Just give me time to save up for a weddin' present. Now, I went to bed early last night and I got to thinkin'. All the murders occurred on a weekday, right?'

'Yes.'

'I don't reckon our bloke's got a regular job, I don't reckon he's got a job at all, right?'

'That may be so.'

'So how's he earn his corn, then?'

'Private income?'

'I'm serious. I've had the incident room run a check on armed crime in the area, check any bullets against the ones we got from the first two murders.'

'I should have thought Mr Davies would already have done that.'

'He did. But they was lookin' for rifles, only rifles, so I suggested they checked all weapons. Who says he's only got a rifle? He might have a bloody tank up his sleeve for all we know, right?'

76

'Well, it is certainly worth looking into.'

'You don't sound very keen on the idea.'

'I have reservations. There has been a certain cold precision about the three murders, almost a kind of detachment from the fact of killing which does not suggest to me that the murderer might be involved in other forms of violent crime. Did you come up with any other ideas?'

'No.'

'Oh.'

'You're the theories man. D'you do any better?'

'I can't claim that. A couple of things have occurred to me though.'

'Like what?'

'Have you had a chance to visit the scenes of the murders?'

'Yes, the first two. Did that yesterday, why?'

'Because having examined the scenes myself I have come to the conclusion that our man is operating on foot. If he has a vehicle he is certainly leaving it a long way from the murder locations.'

'So? I took that for granted. Weren't no tracks, were there? And he wouldn't have left a car on the road where he shot the nurse, it'd've stuck out like a sore thumb, wouldn't it?'

'Exactly.'

'So where does that get us?'

'It confirms the theory that he is local, that he knows the area well. If you want a wild guess, I would say that he does not use a vehicle at all when he is setting out for a kill.'

'So we'll agree on that. Like I said, where does it get us?'

'I am not sure.'

'Marvellous! That all you've got to offer?'

'No. I spoke to Mr Davies yesterday. We had all assumed that our man learnt his shooting with a rifle club, in competition, is that right?'

'What else?'

'What about him being an army reject, a trained sniper, perhaps dismissed when he was found to be mentally unstable?'

'Bit far fetched, ain't it?'

77

'Not really. Think about it. A sniper would have the ideal training for those kind of killings.'

'Maybe you're right. What'd Ewen Davies say?'

He promised to contact the Home Office to make a high-level approach for the information. I doubt we'll get it any other way.'

'A nutty sniper, eh?' Bob said thoughtfully. 'That's a charmin' thought!'

'There was one other thing. I know Mr Davies had enquiries made at rifle clubs, especially the local one, but has he also checked on ex-members? I have in mind people who have moved away from the area, resigned or dropped out of membership lately.'

'D'you ask him?'

'No.'

'Then you'd better do that.'

'I will. And that's about all, so far.'

'Okay, we'd best get on with it I suppose. Back to the grind. Reckon I'd better start on a round of the pubs . . . what're you grinnin' at?'

'I should not have thought that you would find visiting a succession of public houses such a hardship.'

'Well, I'm not goin' to *enjoy* it, am I?'

'No?'

'Not the same, is it? Not the same when you're forced to drink. Like prostitutes, same with them.'

'Pardon?'

'I mean, they don't *enjoy* it with their clients, do they? It's work, they don't *enjoy* it. They only enjoy it when they do it for free with a bloke they chose, don't they? Same with drinkin'. Even Glenfiddich don't taste the same when you're *forced* to drink it.'

'But you will try to give the impression you are enjoying it, for the sake of your cover, will you not?' Leo suggested, hiding a grin behind his hand.

'Oh, yes,' Bob said. 'I'll put on an act, 'course I will . . .'

The killer had laid out a blanket on the floor and was squatting in front of it in the process of inserting a 4 by 2-inch patch of flannel into the top of a two-part cleaning rod. He had completely dismantled the rifle and its parts were laid out in precise order in front of him, each protected from the fibres of the blanket by a piece of clean cotton sheet. To one side was a can of Young's .303 cleaner and a phospher-bronze brush.

Ten candles placed strategically round the outside of the blanket gave a flickering yellow light by which he worked. He would have preferred to work in better light but was not prepared to take the risk that that entailed. The cleaning of the rifle was a ritual that he attended to fastidiously and from which he derived great pleasure. There was an almost sensual delight in handling the exquisitely worked metal that glinted dully in the candlelight. He had spent many hours personalizing this weapon, especially smoothing the bolt action by working it in with a fine grinding paste. There had been more hours spent on the ammunition, cleaning each round, polishing it with a soft cloth and ensuring it was stored dry and dust-free until wanted for use.

The killer handled the rifle with the gentle touch of the lover, for him it was an eminently desirable thing, a thing of powerful personality, magnetic attraction and exquisite beauty. A man might fail such a weapon as this but the rifle would never fail him. It was for him to constantly strive to emulate the perfection the rifle achieved and in the end only more practice, more killing, could lead him towards that goal.

He gave thought then to his future tactics. It was important that he retained the initiative, did not allow his killings to fall into an identifiable pattern. Perhaps this was the time to select random targets rather than those he had pre-selected for variety and degree of difficulty. There was a definite attraction in going out blind, looking for a target of opportunity, pitting his wits and expertise against chance.

He found the prospect immensely exciting. There was something quite exquisitely beautiful in the concept of a totally unplanned encounter when speed would be of the essence if he were to succeed. That was what he would do from now on, accept only those targets that fate offered.

When he had finished cleaning the rifle and had reassembled and repacked it in its carrying case he rummaged in his rucksack for his Ordnance Survey map. If he began to prepare immediately he could set out in the morning for the next shoot.

As he studied the map he switched on his transistor radio and turned it down low. He was not interested in the music. He was waiting for the news bulletin. He liked to hear the guarded statements of the police, the wild speculation of the reporters, to hear public recognition of his expertise.

He recalled his surprise when he first heard himself described as a psychotic killer, and his faint amusement at the stupidity of the police and the press for so depicting him.

Perhaps, though, in time, even they would understand.

Leo arrived back at Dhys-Gla without any clear idea of how he would spend the rest of the day. He went straight to the telephone in the hall and dialled the incident room number. Detective Chief Superintendent Davies was out so he asked for Sergeant Richards.

As he was waiting for Richards to answer, Nerys appeared from the kitchen dressed in faded and torn jeans, a shapeless jumper and a flour-dusted pinafore. He smiled and blew her a kiss but she just looked startled and darted upstairs.

When Sergeant Richards answered Leo passed on to him his enquiry regarding any ex-members of the local rifle club that there might be and asked how things were going on the most recent killing.

'Nothing doing, sir,' Richards answered. 'Got away clean as a whistle, he did, same as last time.'

'Have they finished work at the scene yet?' Leo asked.

'Yes, sir. Wasn't much to do really.'

'Perhaps I will have a look myself this afternoon. Thanks, Gwyn.'

Leo replaced the receiver, walked down the hall and poked his head round the kitchen door. Morwenna was the sole occupant of the room but the table was already laid for the midday meal.

'Didn't expect you back,' Morwenna said accusingly. 'We're

having lunch early, see, all going shopping this afternoon. I was to leave you something cold, I was, just in case.'

'Please do not worry on my account, Morwenna,' Leo said. 'I will do whatever is easiest for you.'

'Then you'll take lunch with the rest of us at twelve.'

Leo grinned. 'Yes, ma'am,' he said. 'I shall be in my room. By the way, where did Nerys rush off to?'

'No idea, I'm sure. Been acting like a looney lamb these last few days. You should do something about it.'

'What can I do?' Leo protested.

'If you don't know I'm sure it's not for me to tell you, is it? Now, go and leave me in peace, man, there's work to be done.'

Leo went to his bedroom, washed, then sat on the wide window-sill, staring out across the valley, until it was time for lunch. He felt vaguely guilty, as if he should be taking some more active role in the investigation than he had so far. But what more could he do until some lead presented itself? Rushing about the countryside looking busy would produce no more rapid results than careful evaluation of the few facts available and the construction of logical theories. Or was he making an excuse for idleness? Had Dhys-Gla infected him with the sloth of the lotus eaters?

When he joined the family in the kitchen he noticed that Nerys had removed her glasses, combed her hair, applied a little make-up and was wearing a becoming woollen dress, presumably in honour of the afternoon's shopping trip. She made no explanation for her earlier behaviour, chattered away as if nothing had occurred.

After the meal Leo helped to clear away the plates, then the family scattered to prepare for their weekly outing. Nerys remained with him in the kitchen.

'What are you going to do this afternoon?' she asked.

Leo took both her hands in his. 'I intend to visit the scene of the last shooting,' he said.

He felt her hands stiffen in his. 'Do you have to?' she asked.

'Yes.'

'Why?'

'How can I write about something I have never seen?'

Her eyes clouded and she looked away.

'Nerys?'

'Yes?'

'What is it?'

'Nothing. Will you be back for dinner tonight?'

'Yes, I expect so.'

'We shall be back at five, will you be back by then?'

'Perhaps. Perhaps a little later. You have no need to worry.'

'I'm not worried. Why should I be worried?'

Leo leant forward and kissed her on the cheek. She did not respond. 'That's fine then,' Leo said.

'You *will* take care, though . . .'

Then the others returned to the kitchen and bore her away in a chorus of goodbyes. He watched them drive off, then went to his bedroom to collect his coat. On his way back down the stairs he recalled something Morwenna had said earlier, something about looney lambs. It sparked off a train of thought and he stopped by the telephone on his way out and dialled the incident room number again. After a brief wait Chief Superintendent Davies came to the phone.

'Any luck, sir?' Leo asked.

'Nothing, Leo. Damn all. You been there?'

'I shall go now.'

'Something you wanted, was there?'

'I just wanted to check one matter with you, sir. I was wondering about the mental institutions in the area . . .'

'Done that, boy. They've got no one missing.'

'Did the chaps check on the list of voluntary patients, and those attending for daily treatment only?'

'Don't remember, to be honest. They should have, but I'll make sure they did. Got something in mind, have you?'

'No, sir. Just a general thought. Clutching at straws, I suppose.'

Or trying to look busy, Leo thought wryly as he replaced the receiver.

When Bob Staunton returned to The Yellow Fox he found Alf King bottling up in the bar, hefting full crates as if they weighed nothing.

'See he's bin at it again,' Alf said by way of greeting.

'Who's that?'

'This nutcase what's shootin' people. Some poor farmer bloke copped it yesterday, didn't he? Heard it on the tranny.'

'Oh, yeah, that's right Alf.'

'Ill wind and all that I suppose . . .'

'What?'

'Well, keeps you in a job, eh? I mean, I'm not being funny or nothin' but it's right, ain't it? Sells papers a thing like this, don't it?' Alf explained.

'Suppose it does, Alf. People say how terrible it all is and that but they still want to read about it. Funny old lot, aren't we?'

'Yeah, be a great world if it weren't for the people in it.'

'Alf, you got such a thing as a list of the local pubs? Not all of 'em, just the ones in Bala and between here and Ffestiniog, say.'

'What's up?' Alf asked, frowning. 'Gone off us, have yer?'

'Don't talk wet. Got a little bit of heaven here, ain't you? I just want to get around 'em, see if I can drum up a story.'

'Had me worried there for a minit. No . . . ain't got a list, but I can write 'em down for you if you like. You want it now?'

'No. I've got to go out again. I'll pick it up at lunchtime, if that's okay?'

'No bother.'

'Okay, mate. Thanks. See you later.'

Bob left Alf King to his labours and drove to the scene of the latest shooting at Migneint. There was not a soul in sight and the high moorland looked bleak and uninviting. He did not even bother to get out of his car, he knew there was nothing here that would help him.

Over lunch at The Yellow Fox he collected the list of public houses from Alf King and, for want of something better to do, set out in his car to inspect them, striking off the list all those that seemed evident tourist traps and therefore unlikely to be the haunt of local residents.

He returned to Bala for his evening meal, then began his pub crawl with those premises furthest from Bala, gradually working his way back to his base. Bob found the evening unrewarding and far from enjoyable. Unrewarding because few of the locals were prepared to encourage him into their conversation on first sight and less than enjoyable because using the car limited him to drinking only half-pints of beer.

At ten o'clock he found himself at The Stag, a small, isolated public house on the road that followed the southern shore of Bala Lake, only a few miles from Bala itself. In the car park were at least twenty motor-cycles and when he entered the small bar he discovered that half of it was occupied by the leather-jacketed riders, laughing, drinking, jostling each other and conducting conversations at the tops of their voices.

Under any other circumstances Bob would have walked straight out again. Drinking with the wheeled gestapo was not for him. As it was, he found himself a stool at the other end of the bar and, forgetting himself, ordered a Glenfiddich.

'We don't have that, sir,' the thin-chested, elderly publican said. 'Plenty of other brands, though.'

Bob sighed. It was one of those nights. 'As it comes then, mate,' he said.

Whilst the landlord was dispensing his drink from the optic Bob looked round the bar. In the centre of the raucous motor-cycle gang was a back that he could hardly fail to recognize. 'Ace' was conspicuous by his size, the length of his greasy black hair, his loud voice and the nickname blazoned arrogantly across the back of his leather jacket. Bob was no coward but even to him this seemed no time to bring up the subject of courtesy on the road, so he contented himself with a grunt of disgust and a scowl that paraded his antagonism but went unobserved.

As the landlord returned with Bob's order, 'Ace' swaggered to the bar counter and stared belligerently towards the two older men, banging his pint glass on the counter to attract attention.

'Here, Ifor, let's have some service here, then!' he demanded.

'I'll come back for the money in a minute,' Ifor said to Bob, hastily pushing the drink across the counter and scuttling down the bar. 'Yes, Jimmy?' he asked timidly.

'Twenty-one pints, and make it fast, see?'

As Ifor set about his task 'Ace' leant on the counter and stared arrogantly at Bob, inviting some comment on his behaviour, waiting for a contentious word. But Bob gritted his teeth and looked away, sipping his drink between set lips. There were distinct disadvantages to working under cover and one of them was that you had to swallow insults from the likes of this smelly little creep. Ifor was bustling about fulfilling the mammoth order, smiling obsequiously, eager to please. Getting no response from Bob, 'Ace' turned away with a contemptuous grin and began feeding the full glasses of beer back to his gang. When the order was complete he pulled out a thick wad of notes and peeled off the top two, throwing them on the counter as if they were scrap paper and accepting the change as if he were granting a favour.

'Have a drink, Ifor,' Bob said when the landlord came back down the bar to take his money. 'You look as if you could do with one.'

The landlord accepted with alacrity and brought his half-pint of beer over to join Bob when he had taken the money. 'Your good health, then,' he said. 'On holiday, are you?'

'Freelance reporter,' said Bob easily. 'These shootings, you know?'

'Oh, yes. Terrible business, terrible business. You know Dai Morgan, that farmer that was shot yesterday?'

'Yeah?'

'Third cousin to my wife, he was.'

'Heard any rumours?' Bob asked.

'About the shooting?'

'Yeah.'

'Not really.'

'I thought it'd be, thought all the locals'd be talkin' about it, ain't that right?'

'Well, people talk about it, but no one can say much, can they? I mean, no one knows anything about it, do they? Anyway, not many of the locals come in at the moment, see.'

'Why's that, Ifor?'

Ifor gestured discreetly towards the other end of the bar. 'Don't like the company, see?' He lit up a cigarette and immediately went into a paroxysm of coughing.

'Can't say I blame them,' Bob commented.

The landlord patted himself on the chest and the coughing fit subsided. 'Shouldn't do it,' he said. 'Damned things always make me cough. Be the death of me, I shouldn't wonder.' He took a swig of his beer, then went back to the cigarette.

'Why d'you put up with them?' Bob asked. 'Get the police, kick 'em out.'

'Oh yes, and what then? Can't have the police here all the time, can I? What if they came back when the police weren't here?'

'If they cause bother, call the police again, get 'em nicked. They'll soon get the idea.'

Ifor shook his head. 'They'll move on eventually. They drink in one place for a while, then they get fed up and move on. Better let them be, isn't it? Anyway, they cause no trouble, see. Bit loud they are, but no real trouble.'

'But they've driven all your local trade away.'

Ifor shrugged. 'They spend more money than the locals. Not short of money, any of them, and they do spend it.'

'Yeah. I saw that big slob flashing his wad about.'

'Talk quietly,' Ifor urged. 'He might hear you.'

'Who is he, anyway? The one reckons he's an ace?'

'Jimmy Bennett.'

'And how come he's so flush? Where's he get his money?'

'He's a contract plasterer. Earns a fortune, he does.'

'That what he told you?'

'That's what he told me.'

'Reckon that's the truth?'

'Don't know, I'm sure. He does seem to be around a lot mid-week but I just thought he didn't work set hours, see.'

'That bastard ain't workin',' Bob said, 'more likely he's dippin' his fingers in the till somewhere.'

'None of my business,' said Ifor. 'Keep to myself, I do. Best way when all's said and done, isn't it?'

86

'Ah well,' Bob said, 'let's have a drink and change the subject. How come you don't stock Glenfiddich . . .?'

Twenty minutes later Bob left, considering that he had done his work for the evening and was justified in retiring to The Yellow Fox and having a nightcap in more congenial company.

As the door closed behind him Jimmy Bennett picked up the remains of his pint and lounged up to the bar.

'Here . . . Ifor. Come here, sod you.'

'Yes, Jimmy?' Ifor enquired, smiling ingratiatingly.

'Who was that old deadbeat, then?'

Ifor shrugged. 'Stranger, Jimmy. Said he was a reporter, here about these shootings, see.'

'Bloody snoopers. What'd he want then?'

'He was just having a drink, Jimmy.'

'And asking questions, I'll bet.'

'Well, yes . . .'

'About us, about me? I saw him looking . . .'

'Well, he did ask who you were . . .'

'And you told him, did you?'

'Yes . . . no harm, was there?' Ifor asked timidly.

Bennett leaned forward and poured the remains of his drink over the landlord's head. 'In a *good* pub, Ifor,' he said, savagely, 'the landlord keeps his mouth *shut*, see?'

Bob was only a mile along the lonely minor road that led back to Bala when he saw the phalanx of lights coming up behind him. For a moment he was nonplussed, then he heard the throaty roar of the motor-cycle engines as the riders closed up on him, riding three abreast, occupying the whole width of the road, their headlights illuminating the inside of his car and dazzling him through his rear-view mirror.

There could be no doubt that these tactics were deliberately intended to unnerve him. Bob swore violently but realized his impotence and kept an even speed and a steady course. Even he, however, was not immune to the implied menace of the solid formation of heavy machines that sat on his tail like a pack of trained dogs, waiting obediently for the order to cut loose.

87

On the first stretch of straight road six of the machines blasted past him on his offside and formed up across the road ahead of him. Then they gradually began to slow down, forcing him to stop.

Bob quickly locked the car doors from the inside, engaged first gear and held one foot on the clutch, the other on the accelerator. If the worst came to the worst he would have no compunction about using the car as a weapon. For all his determination he felt suddenly very alone. But the riders made no move. Those ahead did not even turn to look at him. They just sat there astride their machines, immobile except for a slight movement of the wrist as they revved up their engines and let them die back in unison, a sudden crescendo of sound followed by a low throbbing, repeated time after time until it became a torture, playing on the nerves, eating away at sanity.

Then Bennett rode up and stopped beside the closed driver's window of the car. He sat staring at Bob, and his very immobility was a threat. He did nothing, said nothing.

Bob wound down his window a fraction and opened his mouth to warn his tormentor that he was not a man to be trifled with. Bennett opened the throttle of his machine and the noise of the engine drowned Bob's words. Twice more Bob tried to speak, twice more Bennett silenced him with harsh screams of the powerful engine. Bob gripped the steering wheel with hands that shook with what he thought was anger. Bennett was grinning fiercely now, showing small, uneven teeth, the smile of the bully sure of his victory.

Suddenly he leant sideways and spat at Bob. The spittle struck and slid down the driver's window. It was so unexpected that Bob's foot slid from the clutch and the car jolted forward, then stalled.

Then there was a vicious blast of noise and, as one, the riders accelerated away into the night, leaving a vacuum of silence behind them.

CHAPTER SEVEN

At 8 a.m. the following morning Bob Staunton was called from his breakfast to take a telephone call in the kitchen of The Yellow Fox. Having to leave his first meal of the day unfinished did nothing to improve his temper, still frayed from his unfortunate and disturbing confrontation with the motor-cycle brigade the night before. He had tried to put the matter from his mind, it was irrelevant to the job in hand, but he was conscious that he had come out of the affair second best and that irritated him beyond measure.

Being bested by one of 'the great unwashed', and a Nazi lover to boot, was not a matter Bob Staunton could take lightly, especially since the preservation of his cover prevented him from saying or doing anything about it. The wound had festered during half a dozen medicinal Glenfiddichs the night before and he had woken with his head still throbbing with the insult to his personal and professional dignity. Consequently when he picked up the receiver, his enquiry was less than encouraging.

'Yeah?'

'Bob?'

'Right.'

'Ewen Davies.'

'Ah, sorry, Ewen mate, didn't know it was you.'

'Nearly bit my head off, boy. Who'd you think was calling, the Inland Revenue?'

'Just one of those mornin's. What's up?'

'Not a lot. But I think we should meet. I've got answers to some of the matters you and Leo raised.'

'Okay, mate. When and where?'

'There's a layby on the Bala to Trawsfynydd Road, beside Llyn Celyn . . .'

'Clyn what?'

'Lake Celyn, on the map it's shown as Llyn Celyn, 'Llyn' is Welsh for 'lake', see?'

'Oh, yeah, bit slow this mornin'.'

'I'll see you there at . . . say ten?'

'Right. No bother.'

'You'll ring Leo?'

'Yeah . . . listen, see yer later,' Bob said hurriedly, 'must go, me egg's gettin' cold.'

The three cars lined up behind each other in the layby and Bob and Leo joined Chief Superintendent Davies in his slightly larger vehicle.

'Mornin' Ewen,' Bob said. 'How's your belly off for spots?'

'Your mood has improved radically since I spoke to you earlier,' Davies commented.

'Yeah, that Glynis. What a good girl she is.'

'Glynis?'

'Landlord's wife. Halfway through me breakfast I was when you called, so she sees it's gettin' cold, whips the plate away and cooks up a new lot. Heart of gold that woman. Wouldn't get service like that in a modern hotel would you?'

Davies laughed. 'Maybe you're right, Bob. Keep your bed warm as well, does she?'

'I leave all that to him,' Bob said, pointing at Leo. 'Now, what you got for us?'

Davies took out a sheaf of papers stapled together and read from the notes he had made.

'Your enquiry about local mental homes, Leo. We were

already covering these, there are no resident patients missing and so far as is possible we have checked all recent releases and also the out-patients. Really none of them are even remotely likely. You asked about other crimes where guns had been used, Bob. Well, we've had two murders with guns in this area in the last three years but both men are still in custody so they're ruled out. There have been three bank raids in the last year, quite heavy, they got twenty thousand from one, and two bank employees have been killed. No arrests so far.'

'What sort of guns?' Bob asked.

'The usual. Sawn-off shotguns. Only thing is, the reports say the killings were unnecessary. In both cases cashiers were killed after the villains had the money, and they weren't trying to stop them getting away either.'

'Charmin',' Bob commented.

'But in one case there was no killing. Were all three done by the same team?' Leo put in.

'Same team. In the first job they fired at a girl but she recovered.'

'No ident?' Bob asked.

'Nothing. They wore stocking masks. No ideas either. They only hit small local branch banks. Crime Squad reckons it's a new team.'

'How many in the team?' Bob asked.

'Just two men.'

'What about the cars they used?' Leo asked.

'Stolen on the day of the raids. So far no one has seen them transferring vehicles either. Only thing is, the raid at Harlech, that's the only one outside our own area of search, on that one there was a witness, a young lad saw two men roughly answering the description of the raiders riding off on a trials bike, but it was two streets away from where the stolen car was dumped and it might not have been them. Anyway, he didn't get the index number.'

'What's a trials bike?' Bob asked.

'Motor-bike. One of them with thick tyres and high mud-guards, used for cross-country trials riding.'

'Not like the ones them Hell's Angels use?'

'No. Why d'you ask?'

'Nothin'. Just thinkin'. You was sayin'?'

'That's about all.' He turned over a page. 'Your army enquiry, Leo, about the snipers . . . I contacted the Home Office and they asked for a written report, which I've sent off. Told them it was urgent but you know what it's like, probably take days before they get back to us. I'll let you know when they do. Next . . . enquiries at the local rifle club . . . yes, here we are, we went back five years . . . in that time two members moved out of the area, a John Walters and a David Owens. Both joined rifle clubs elsewhere and have been eliminated in the course of the general enquiries we had made at all clubs in the U.K. One man resigned, a Major Thomas, lives near Penmachno, he's not been seen yet . . .'

'I have met him,' Leo said. 'He is a personal friend of the family I am lodging with. Not a likely candidate but I will interview him.'

'Right, I'll leave that to you. There was one other chap, local lad named James Bennett, he was required to leave the club two years ago. Officially it was for what they called persistently poor range discipline, but there was also some question of a theft of cash from the clubrooms. No address for him but no doubt it won't take long to track him down.'

'How old is he, this James Bennett?' Bob asked.

'He'd be in his late twenties, something of a layabout I gather, didn't mix in well at the rifle club, why?'

Bob was grinning hugely. 'I think I've already found him.'

'Yes?'

'Yeah, a right saucy bastard. I'll tell you a little story . . . yesterday mornin' I was drivin' along, mindin' me own business, when this two-wheeled bandit done up like Hermann Goering cuts me up, see? It so happens I catches up with him in Bala 'cos the road's blocked and I get a good look at 'im. Anyway, that night I'm out doin' me round of pubs and I finish up at a place called The Stag, back of Bala Lake. When I get there, there's this same finger with about twenty of his mates, like a meetin' of the Hitler bloody youth it was. I tell you if that lot is your citizens of tomorrow then we've got bother . . . anyway, I gets chattin' to the landlord, puny little fellah but okay enough, and I see this stormtrooper flashin' a great wad of notes, must have been a couple of hundred quid, so I naturally enquires who he is . . . and it so happens his name's Jimmy Bennett. How about that, then?'

'Bit of luck that, boy,' Davies said. 'I'll send someone down to the pub at lunchtime to try and get an address for him.'

'Don't bother,' Bob said. 'It'll make my day to do it meself. I didn't tell you the rest.'

'What's that?'

'After I left the pub this Bennett must've strapped the landlord, found out I was askin' questions. I'm a mile down the road and all of a sudden they're all round me, trying to put the frighteners on.'

'What happened?' Leo asked anxiously.

'Not much. They tried it on, you know, playin' the big silent routine, didn't bother me none. Mind you, if it'd been an ordinary bloke they'd have scared the pants off him. Anyway, after a bit this Bennett spits on me car, dirty bastard, and they all clear off. So it'll give me great pleasure to personally pull his legs from under him. Good suspect, ain't he?'

'For what?' Leo asked.

'Eh?'

'Are you saying that he is a suspect for the bank raids or our murders, or both?'

'Both, mate.'

'How do you come to that conclusion then, Bob?' Davies asked.

'Take the bank raids first. There was a motor-bike used in them, right?'

'Maybe,' Davies said. 'A trials bike, maybe.'

'Okay, maybe. Then this Bennett is in possession of a pile of cash, then he tries to scare me off when he discovers I'm askin' questions about him, why? I'll tell you, he's a villain and a nasty one at that. Then on top of that he knows about rifles because he was in the rifle club and got kicked out and why did he get kicked out? For indiscriminate shootin', or something like that, right? So don't tell me he ain't the best suspect we've had so far.'

'We have had no other suspects at all so far,' Leo pointed out.

'Exactly,' Bob said emphatically, as if this was a complete answer.

'I wonder . . . you don't happen to know if this Bennett was ever in the army, do you, sir?' Leo enquired of Davies.

Davies shook his head. 'No idea.'

'What's this obsession you've got with the army, Leo?' Bob complained.

'Have you visited the scene of the last shooting?'

'Yeah.'

'The killer was on flat open ground but he got to within 200 yards of the farmer, two dogs and a flock of sheep, and killed his man, all without being detected. That suggests to me that he had training in fieldcraft.'

'So? When we capture Bennett maybe we'll find he's been in the cake, will that make you happy?'

'I would be happier if that were so.'

'Look, mate. Bennett is all we've got. He might not be much but he's as good as ours, stand on me. So if it turns out he's white as the driven snow, what do we lose?'

'Time,' Leo said.

The killer had decided not to take food with him and was preparing a meal before he left. Although it was cold outside, the temperature in the small enclosed living area was kept up by the portable stove, fed by butane gas containers, which served both for cooking and heating purposes. The stove and gas containers, like all the other stores, he had accumulated over the last year, stocking up with a few items at a time. He had taken care over this part of the operation, buying in small lots in different towns and always returning to his base at night and by different routes. His quarters were not comfortable but they were secure and although his diet was rather monotonous it was sufficient and in

94

any event, he was not used to an abundance of personal comforts.

The only item which he had not brought with him was the low, wooden frame bed, which he had made himself from materials found on the spot. It was his sole concession to comfort. He was fortunate that drinking water was readily available, although he took the precaution of adding a purifying tablet before he drank it. His toilet facilities were primitive. He boiled water in a saucepan in which to wash and shave and, like the desert soldier, took a shovel with him out into the open when nature called.

The small room was heavy with the strong, sickly sweet smell of his body odour, for although he washed his body regularly, he never changed his clothes. He had from the start garbed himself to face inclement weather and his clothing was vitally important to the success of his shooting, it had to be comfortable and not restrain him, yet offer him warmth and protection. Having found the right combination of garments whilst practising with the rifle, it was important that he wore no others when he was shooting, and since he had no facility for washing or dry-cleaning them, they had inevitably become stained with his sweat.

It did not occur to him that the time space between his killings was shrinking, that the pace of his killings was gradually increasing, that the need to test himself and his weapon was occurring more often. He ate slowly, savouring both the food and the kill to come, staring into the middle distance with a vacant smile on his face. He did not know that he was insane.

Bob and Leo parked side by side in the car park at The Stag, then Leo went and sat in the passenger seat of Bob's car as they waited for the public house to open.

'You know what?' Bob said, 'I'm starvin'.'

'But you had breakfast not long ago,' Leo protested.

'A man needs good honest sustenance,' Bob said. 'You know what's wrong with this country, I mean, what's behind it all? Dieting. That's what it is.'

'How do you come to that conclusion?'

'Easy. Half the country's on a diet of one sort or another, right? It debilitates you mate, that's what it does. Weakens the body and the mind, makes you give in too quick, take the easy way out. Now a man with a full belly, he's ready for anything, right? History proves I'm right.'

'History?'

'Take Neville Chamberlain. I bet he was on a diet.'

Leo was lost. 'Chamberlain? Why should you think that?'

'I'll tell you mate, if he'd had a good solid meal inside him when he went to Munich he'd never have come back wavin' that bit of paper and prattlin' on about peace in our time, would he? Stands to reason.'

'Does it?'

'Certainly. So what happens? We went to war anyway, mate, that's what happened. So much for Chamberlain and his diet. And who got us out of the mix? Churchill, that's who. Now *there* was a man never went on a diet in his life. What a good trencherman *he* was. There was a man what *knew* what to do with a plate of good grub!'

'So you think the only qualification for being Prime Minister is having a large capacity for food?'

'No, but it'd help. You'd get the right sort of bloke then, not like some of the wishy-washy poofs we've had since the war.'

Leo, aware that he could never win an argument when faced with Bob's convoluted and illogical thinking, decided to steer the conversation in another direction.

'James Bennett,' he said.

'Eh? What about him?'

'I did not want to say too much in front of Mr Davies but he does not strike me as being a prime suspect for our murders.'

'Why not?'

'He's not the type.'

'Brilliant!'

'You described him as a yobbo, a layabout. No doubt from what we have learned about him you are right. If that is so it is hard for me to see him in the role of the cold, calculating, undoubtedly insane killer who is a world-class shot and a master of fieldcraft.'

'There are times, Leo, when you are about as much help to me as five legs to a dog. You have a talent for misery, you know that? You don't eat enough, that's your trouble.'

'I am just worried that we may be wasting valuable time on a dead end.'

'Nobody asked you to come here, did they? You invited yourself. If you're so worried, you push off and tear round the mountains lookin' for clues. Me? I'm goin' after this Jimmy Bennett. Go on, push off!'

'I'd rather not, actually. You just might decide to tackle this Bennett on your own and that could be dangerous.'

'You think I'm dim, don't you?'

Leo smiled. 'No . . . just occasionally impulsive and always fearless.'

'Get stuffed!' said Bob, grinning.

'I have good news for you,' Leo said.

'That makes a change!'

'The Stag has just opened its doors.'

The landlord looked surprised to see customers waiting on his doorstep and seemed uneasy when he recognized Bob Staunton.

'Remember me, Ifor?' Bob asked. 'I was in last night.'

'Yes . . . of course . . .'

Bob indicated Leo. 'Mate of mine,' he said.

'A charming house you have, Ifor,' Leo said.

Ifor smiled uncertainly.

'You got any grub, Ifor?' Bob asked.

'Well . . . a sandwich, or I could warm up a meat pie?'

Bob sighed. 'Not exactly what I had in mind, but it'll do,' he said.

'Which? Cheese sandwich or meat pie?'

'Both,' Bob said, 'and two glasses of that cookin' Scotch you gave me last night.'

Leo winced but Ifor only nodded and disappeared into the back kitchen.

'You could have left poor Ifor a little of his pride,' Leo suggested mildly.

Bob was adamant. 'He opened his mouth last night, set me up for Bennett and his gang. You want me to fall on his neck? Not likely. Weak as water he is.'

'Perhaps he is on a diet,' Leo suggested, grinning.

'More than likely,' Bob said. 'More than likely, son.'

He munched his way determinedly through the food Ifor provided before broaching the subject of Jimmy Bennett.

'We're in trouble, Ifor,' he said.

'Trouble?' Ifor repeated anxiously.

'We need copy . . . we need a story.'

Ifor looked relieved. 'But I thought you said you were reporting on the murders?'

'Right. Trouble is, no one knows anythin', do they? The police seem to be sittin' about on their fannies . . . nothing to write about, is there?'

'I'm sure *I* can't help you . . .'

'Maybe you can. I've got this idea, could be good. Bit of human interest, right? What we do is get these lads what was in here last night, the motor-bike lot, you know? Get them to run about the roads helpin' to look for the murderer, with me?'

'But the police . . .?'

'It ain't nothin' to do with the police. The lads are just citizens doin' their duty, right? I can see the headlines now, "Hell's Angels Hunt Murderer", "Motor-Bike Heroes Turn Detective", great stuff, bound to get front page in all the nationals, that.'

'I don't think those boys would want to do it . . .' Ifor said hesitantly.

'Don't know till we ask 'em, do we?' Bob pressed. 'I never met anyone yet who didn't want to get their name in the paper. Could be good for you as well.'

'How?'

'We get a photographer down, right? Pictures of the lads out huntin' on their bikes, parked in your car park here lookin' at maps, maybe in the bar havin' a drink with you servin' 'em with a

98

big smile, make sure we get the name of the pub in, eh? What would that do for your trade?'

Bob and Leo watched as avarice chased the fear from Ifor's eyes. But he was still uncertain. He had obviously been warned not to talk about Bennett and his gang but the carrot now dangled before him was eminently inviting.

'You'd have to speak to Jimmy Bennett,' he said cautiously. 'It's not up to me.'

'Okay,' Bob said casually, 'where can we find him?'

'He'll probably be here tonight. If not, tomorrow night.'

'Too late. We've got deadlines to meet. Where's he work? We'll go and see him.'

'I don't know where he works.'

'Okay, where's he live, then?'

'I don't think I should say . . .' Ifor said uncertainly.

Bob shrugged. 'Then the deal's off. Now or never, mate. That's the way it is in our business. Today's big news is tomorrow's two lines. Pity. Jimmy might not be pleased when he knows what you turned down for him.'

Ifor chewed that over for a moment, then came to a decision. 'Two miles down this road . . .' he began.

'Towards Bala?' Leo asked.

Ifor pointed. 'No, the other way. There's a track on your left, leads up to a small farm, you can't miss it, there's a big old dead oak tree on the corner. Half a mile up there is another track on your right. Jimmy lives in a caravan at the end of the track.'

'Ifor,' Bob said, 'you've just done yourself a very big favour.'

Leo led the way along the narrow, twisting road that followed the shoreline of Bala Lake until he found the turn-off beside the dead oak. The track was wide but rutted by the tyres of farm vehicles. It twisted and turned and, by the time Leo found the secondary track on his right, was enclosed by trees. The route to the caravan was no more than a barely defined path through a small forest of conifers, ending at a clearing beside a shallow stream that ran down towards the lake a mile away. At no time had they caught sight of the main farm buildings.

99

The caravan looked to be derelict. The paint had peeled off completely in places exposing bare metal, now stained and pitted with rust, the windows were obscured with the dirt of years and vivid green moss grew on the narrow window-sills. The chimney-stack poking through the tattered roof had rusted almost through and was leaning at a drunken angle and the wooden steps leading up to the door looked positively dangerous.

Bob and Leo got out of their cars and walked forward to try the door. It was locked and there was no reply when they hammered on it for the owner to appear.

'Not exactly Shangri-La, is it?' Bob commented.

'What the estate agents would call "a bijou residence in need of some attention",' Leo suggested.

Leo scrambled up on to a rickety dustbin, wiped a section of the window with his hand and peered inside.

'Anything?' Bob asked, gripping Leo's ankles as if they were both on the north face of the Eiger.

'The place is like a pigsty,' Leo reported. 'Dirty clothes thrown everywhere, unmade bed, empty bottles, last month's washing-up . . .'

'Any sign of a rifle?'

'Who can tell in this mess?'

Leo jumped down and wiped his hand fastidiously on the grass to remove the grime.

'Wouldn't be much good buildin' roads, would you?' Bob commented.

'I am not a navvy, I am a detective.'

'Whoever told you that?'

'May I ask what you propose to do?'

Bob grinned. 'Got a nice clean job for you . . .'

'Really . . .' said Leo suspiciously.

'Drive into Portmadoc, see Davies, tell him to get a warrant to search this place, then come back here with him.'

'And what will you do in the meantime?'

'Thought I'd plant a crop of cannabis while I'm waiting, looks like good soil,' said Bob, scuffling at the ground with his shoe.

'I'm serious!'

'You always are,' Bob sighed. 'I'll tuck me car out of sight, then find a spot where I can see without bein' seen, what else?'

'And if Bennett returns?'

Bob raised his hands skywards in exasperation.

'I hope you won't try to tackle him alone . . .' Leo persisted.

'No chance,' Bob said caustically. 'I'm too much of a coward, I'll wait till he's asleep then run down here and kick hell out of his bloody motor-bike!'

Bob reluctantly began to climb up the steep slope on one side of the clearing. He had chosen this side because the trees seemed to be less dense and the slope steeper, which would give him a better chance of securing a position of advantage from which to view the clearing.

Despite the fact that the sky was overcast and the day by no means warm, by the time Bob had climbed the first hundred feet he was short of breath and sweating from the exertion. Ahead of him was an almost vertical treeless bank topped by a massive flat-topped boulder and after a few more minutes of slithering and sliding and muted Anglo-Saxon expletives he managed to skirt the bank and clamber up on to the rock.

He sat on top of the rock to gather his breath. From here he could see, across the tree-tops, part of the minor road beside the lake, and the lake itself. To his right he had a view of the roofs of the farmhouse and outbuildings. Looking down in front of the rock, he had, by chance, because a dead tree had fallen and cut a swathe through its smaller live brethren, a partial view of the caravan and the clearing in front of it.

It was good enough. He would hear any vehicle approaching anyway and no doubt if he stood up he would have an even better view. For the moment he sat where he was, waiting for his chest to stop heaving. He wondered about Leo. The lad was not himself, had been out of sorts since soon after they arrived. It had been easier than usual to bait him and he seemed to have a vacant look in his eyes, as if he were present in body but not in mind. He wondered if the joke he had made with Leo about the girl at the farm had been nearer the truth than he imagined. Had

Leo Wyndsor finally met his match? On balance Bob hoped he had. An honest woman, strong of mind and body, would do Leo Wyndsor a power of good. He wondered what the girl was like, debated finding an excuse to meet her. He did not want Leo married to some backwoods scrubber who would screw the lad up and ruin his life, he was worth better than that. Yes, he would give this girl the once-over, make sure she was suitable.

That decision made, Bob stood up and moved forward to the edge of the rock. He had a view of the whole clearing now, he could even see the oil stain where Bennett usually parked his motor-bike, and if he moved forward right to the edge he could probably see the front door of the caravan. He stood on the edge of the drop, leaning slightly forward, unaware of the loose stone beneath his left foot.

He felt the bullet strike him but did not hear the whipcrack of the shot until he was hurtling forward in mid-air and even then he did not realize what had happened.

His body plunged down the bank, rolled and tumbled downwards through the trees until brought suddenly to a jarring halt by a solid tree trunk. He lay still, blood weeping slowly through the hair on the back of his head.

To his amazement he was alive and conscious. He did not move, did not even dare open his eyes. There was no way the killer would miss with a second shot.

CHAPTER EIGHT

When Leo Wyndsor arrived back at the caravan, followed by Chief Superintendent Davies and three detectives in another car, he saw Bob Staunton sitting on the grass at the side of the clearing holding a handkerchief to the back of his head and looking as if he had just been pulled through a hedge backwards.

Leo and Davies ran across to him.

'Are you all right, Bob?' Leo asked anxiously.

'Fine. Bruised ribs, a bit of a headache,' Bob answered, still too shaken to find an acid reply.

'What happened?' Davies asked, indicating the bloodied handkerchief.

'Fell off a rock back there,' Bob said. 'I reckon the Good Lord looks after his own,' he added, wiping his bloodstreaked hands on his jacket.

'Meaning what?' Davies enquired.

'Meanin' the same moment I fell off that bloody rock some bastard took a pot-shot at me with a rifle ... just creased the back of me head ... and I ain't open to bets as to who it was!'

'Bennett?' Davies suggested.

'Who else?'

'You saw him?' Leo put in.

'Nope. Didn't see nobody, too busy falling down that bank,

bloody nearly unconscious, wasn't I? Anyway I had a look round when I come to a bit, but no sign, nothin'.'

It did not seem appropriate to Bob to tell the others that he had been too scared to move for at least two minutes, during every second of which time he had confidently expected a bullet to smash into his body.

'So it might not have been Bennett,' Leo pointed out.

'Got any better ideas?' Bob asked querulously.

'Not at the moment. We had better have a doctor look at you.'

'Not likely. Only nicked me on the back of the head, didn't he? You got the search warrant, Ewen?'

'Yes, but . . .'

'But nothin'. Get on the car radio, put a team up in those trees back there. With a bit of luck the bullet will've lodged somewhere we can find it. Whilst you're about it send a posse up to the farm, it's up the main track further.' He indicated the direction with his thumb. 'They must have heard something, unless they're all stone deaf . . . 'sides they're probably Bennett's landlords, right?'

'I'll do that now.' Davies strode away across the clearing to his car.

Leo offered his hand to help Bob to his feet. 'Are you sure you are all right?' he asked.

'Right enough. Nothin' wrong with me a few minutes alone with Jimmy Bennett won't put right. Stop fussin' Leo, you're like a bloody mother hen.'

'You are suffering from shock and possibly also slight concussion . . .'

'Leo,' Bob interrupted, 'I'll make one concession, right?'

'And what is that?'

'You can kick the door of the caravan in.'

Leo looked down at his recently purchased and expensive shoes. 'If it makes no difference to you,' he said, 'I'll use the tyre lever from the car.'

'You got no sense of the dramatic,' Bob complained.

The caravan door practically fell off its hinges at the sight of the tyre lever. The inside of the caravan was exactly as Leo had described it earlier when he had looked in through the window, a jumble of discarded clothing, beer cans, bottles, dirty crockery and accumulated rubbish. There were only three rooms, a lounge-cum-bedroom at one end, bathroom and toilet in the centre and a tiny kitchen at the other end. In every room was the heavy, repulsive smell of stale sweat.

'No wonder Bennett's a villain,' Bob said, looking round. 'Comes from a deprived home, don't he?'

Leo wrinkled his nose. 'How can anyone live like this? The smell is appalling.'

'Yeah,' Bob agreed, 'maybe no one ever told him he had a personal problem. Better get the lads in, make a start.'

For an hour the officers searched the caravan but they found nothing at all of any interest. Leo sent an officer out to inspect the dustbin, then beckoned Bob into the kitchen and ran some water into the sink.

'I suggest you wash your face before we go any further,' he said.

'What for?'

'You look like a war casualty. I will see if I can find you a half-clean towel.'

'You'll be lucky,' Bob said, inspecting his face in a sliver of mirror stuck up above the sink.

When Bob had tidied himself up they met Davies outside to discuss the next move.

'Better circulate him,' Bob said. ' "Wanted for questioning" will do at the moment.'

'If he did those bank jobs,' Davies said, 'he wasn't wearing his motor-cycle leathers that's for sure, someone would have mentioned it.'

'What was the description of the raider's clothing?' Leo asked.

'Next to nothing. Roughly dressed, the witnesses said. Could mean anything, couldn't it?'

'Could mean he was wearing some of those old clothes lying about in there,' Bob suggested.

'It could,' Davies agreed, 'but on the other hand . . .'

'Shut up!' Bob said suddenly.

'What?'

'Quiet! Listen!'

Then the others heard what Bob's sharp ears had picked up, the distant hum of a motor-cycle engine.

'Surely he's not coming back here!' Davies said.

'Dunno. Wait . . .'

The noise was getting louder. They heard the sound die away, then increase in volume as the rider turned up the track towards the farm.

'Clear out, all of you,' Bob said. 'I want him meself.'

'Bob . . .' Leo began.

'Do as yer told,' Bob shouted, 'I want him, I'm entitled, ain't I?'

Davies nodded to his men and they piled into the cars and drove them out of sight amongst the trees. With the greatest reluctance, Leo went with them.

When Bennett rode into the clearing he saw Bob Staunton standing alone, waiting for him. He stopped, cut the engine, pulled the bike up on to its stand and stepped off it.

'You don't learn very fast, do you old man?' he said. 'How'd you find this place, eh boy? Old Ifor been talking again, has he?'

He undid the strap of his helmet and began to walk towards Staunton, who stood calmly waiting for him.

'You and Ifor, you need a lesson, don't you?' Bennett said, advancing on Bob, swinging the heavy helmet menacingly in his hand. 'I don't like snoopers . . . don't like scruffy old men asking . . .'

He stopped suddenly when he saw the smashed-in door of the caravan. 'What the hell . . .?!'

'I've got news for you, sonny Jim,' Bob said. 'This just ain't your day.'

Bennett rushed him then, swinging the helmet in a wide looping blow aimed at Bob's head. Bob stepped inside the flailing arm and kicked Bennett viciously between the legs. His antagonist dropped to the ground as if he had been poleaxed, squirming into a foetal position, bellowing in pain.

Bob leant down beside the contorted face of the younger man and spoke clearly into his ear.

'Jimmy, you are nicked,' he said. And, in case Bennett was in any doubt, he added, 'and that's official!'

Davies and his officers searched Bennett, finding nothing of immediate interest, then drove him off to Portmadoc to be questioned, leaving Bob and Leo to direct the team due to arrive to search for the bullet fired at Bob earlier and to make enquiries at the farmhouse at the head of the main track.

As they waited, Leo asked: 'Do we go to Portmadoc later to join the interrogation?'

'No, mate, we'll leave that to Ewen Davies. Diplomacy, see. Don't want him to think we're hoggin' the show, do we?'

'I hope he realizes that it could not possibly have been Bennett who shot at you.'

'Bound to, isn't he? He's not that daft. Bennett wasn't surprised to see me alive, was he? He was just surprised to see me there at all. Anyway, Ewen will know Bennett would never have come back here if it had been him, he'd have had it on his toes.'

'Which raises an interesting point.'

'That point bein'?'

'Was it chance that the killer shot at you when you were watching Bennett's caravan or was there some deliberate purpose in it?'

'It weren't no chance, Leo. He was comin' here, sussed who I was, and panicked. It was Bennett's mate, wasn't it? I mean, if it wasn't Bennett, who else could it be?'

'I cannot answer that at the moment.'

'All we've got to do is find the bullet he fired at me, match it to the other killings, then strap Bennett for the name of his mate. It's practically in the bag, me old darlin'. One other thing . . . button yer lip about me gettin' shot at. I told Ewen the same, no word to anybody, specially not the press, that way it gets interestin' if someone shows out he knows about it, right?'

'That only holds good if Bennett was responsible for the bank jobs. If he was, then he has a colleague in crime who could conceivably be our killer I suppose, but if he was not, then not only do we have no lead to the killer but we have assaulted and arrested an innocent man.'

'Innocent?' said Bob, mortally offended. 'That Bennett's about as innocent as Attila the Hun!'

'I am inclined to agree with you. Let us hope we soon come by some evidence to support our opinion. At the moment we would be hard put to convict him of breathing!'

Bob sighed. 'What's this girl's name?' he asked.

'Girl?'

'At the farm where you're stayin'.'

'Oh, Nerys . . . Nerys Johns. Why?'

'Do me a personal favour, Leo. Go and hold her hand, will yer? Breathe in her ear, tell her she's wonderful, anything . . . just so's you leave me in peace.'

'The last time I left you here alone you almost managed to get yourself shot, remember?'

'I promise not to do it again,' Bob said, straightfaced, 'if only you'll go and cook your theories somewhere else.'

'I shall wait until Davies' team arrives,' said Leo determinedly.

Bob walked away towards the trees.

'Where are you going?' Leo called after him.

Bob kept walking but looked back over his shoulder. 'If you'd ever been in the army, you'd never've asked that question,' he said.

When Leo returned to Dhys-Gla at five o'clock Nerys came running out to meet him. She took his arm and led him to the house, chattering on about the minor happenings there during the day. She did not ask him what he had been doing, which surprised Leo a little since in his experience women were always acutely inquisitive.

'We all missed you,' she said at the end of her recital.

'I have only been gone since breakfast,' Leo protested gently. But it was a warming feeling to have Nerys admit that she was included in those who had missed him.

'It seems a lot longer,' Nerys said, then added, changing the subject, 'Red and Merry are getting fat. They need exercise.'

'No doubt they do,' Leo said, 'but they will have to wait, unless you care to ride them round the paddock.'

Nerys made a face. 'They would be insulted,' she said.

'Tell them it is my fault,' Leo grinned.

'I might just do that,' Nerys countered as they entered the house. 'Do you want to take a bath before dinner, then?'

'You think I need to?'

'You do smell a little odd.'

Leo laughed. 'Jolly good job I am not a sensitive soul.'

'Well, it's the truth. You smell like a jumble sale ... old clothes and musty cupboards.'

Leo kissed her on the cheek and started up the stairs. 'That,' he said, 'is not in the least surprising.'

It was the nearest she had come to asking him a question about his activities during the day. He wondered if she would be so controlled if they were married and she had known about the attempt on Bob Staunton's life. Or perhaps it was that she simply was not interested. It might be that she felt nothing more for him than genuine platonic friendship. He found the idea intensely irritating and put it from his mind.

As he lay in the bath he wondered what was happening at the incident room at Portmadoc. What was Jimmy Bennett having to say for himself? Leo was still unhappy in his mind that bank raids and expert and calculated murder went hand in hand. Yet two people had died in the bank raids, gunned down for no reason, the reports said. A man who could do that with a shotgun could presumably be quite capable of a similar act with a rifle.

It seemed to hinge for the moment on whether or not Bennett was one of the two bank raiders. If he was then they had a reasonable lead on the murders. If he was not, then they were back to square one. Without Bennett they had nothing. The only other possible lead, the enquiry concerning ex-snipers, had dead-ended with the Home Office and in any event it was highly speculative.

Leo rose suddenly out of the bath and began to towel himself down. He had no need to wait on the army, at least some of the information he wanted was available nearer to hand.

Daffyd Johns had spent the afternoon with the recently widowed Mrs Morgan and at the evening meal the conversation centred on the difficulty she would face in running the farm now that her husband was dead. It cast a cloud over the family and the meal was a quiet, subdued affair. Nerys said very little, but her eyes hardly left Leo's face, as if she needed constant reassurance that he was there, alive and well.

As they were clearing away the plates Leo asked Nerys for Major Thomas's telephone number.

'You want to see him?' Daffyd interjected. 'He'll be at home, just call there.'

'He won't mind?'

'He'll be glad of the company.'

Nerys saw Leo off. She seemed preoccupied with thoughts of her own. As he drove away she stood by the front door of the farmhouse, watching until the lights of his car disappeared in the darkness that shrouded the trees bordering the track.

Following Daffyd's directions, Leo had no difficulty in locating Major Thomas's house, which was set back from the road just outside Penmachno. It was in fact no more than a cottage with modest gardens bordered at the rear by a shrub-lined stream.

Thomas greeted his unexpected visitor effusively, as glad of the company as Daffyd Johns had predicted he would be. Apart from a daily help, he had lived alone since the death of his wife some five years previously and loneliness, unadmitted but real, had deadened his days. He sat Leo in a comfortable wingback chair beside the fire in the lounge and set glasses and a bottle of whisky on a low wooden table between them.

'I have come to take advantage of your expertise, Major,' Leo admitted as Thomas poured the drinks with a generous hand.

'I don't think we need to be formal, the name is Owen,' Thomas said, settling himself in his chair. 'What exactly did you want to ask me about?'

Leo pointed to the mantelpiece, on which rested a collection of plaques, cups, certificates and trophies. 'I am interested in knowing about shooting, particularly about competition shooting and about snipers.'

'Two quite different things ... you are thinking about the murders, obviously.'

'Yes, Owen. The man has killed at ranges varying from 200 yards up to about 800. In two cases he fired from a static position, which might suggest he was competition trained, but in the other case he used fieldcraft to approach his victim, which is more in the line of the sniper.'

'About snipers I can tell you little, we used them in the last war of course, but since then things have changed, their training has become much more sophisticated. In those days, I can't speak for now, in those days it wasn't necessary for a sniper to be a top-flight shot because we found that more often than not the man who was an expert shot lacked the other essential characteristics. He had to be a competent shot of course, but more important he had to be of even temperament, unexcitable and with a high degree of self-confidence. They were usually loners, men who preferred to work alone, introverted types, non-conformers you might say. You see, these men were hunters, skilled in fieldcraft, taught to get within certain killing range and to extricate themselves afterwards. As a matter of fact we found ex-gamekeepers made damn good snipers.'

'You've read the newspapers, Owen. From what you said at Dhys-Gla last time we met I gathered that you thought he might be a trained sniper, this murderer.'

Thomas sipped his drink and considered the question. 'Yes, I'd be inclined to think that,' he said eventually. 'I gather he got within 200 yards of Dai Morgan before he shot him. They were on open upland with virtually no cover and Dai had good eyes and two damn fine dogs with him. Anyone without training would have needed enormous luck to get away with it.'

'And yet the first two killings were quite different,' Leo prompted.

'Yes, indeed. I think this man must be something rather

special, a trained sniper who also happens to be an expert competition shot.'

'But is he? He took three shots at his first victim and the single shot that killed the nurse could have been lucky,' Leo said, interested to see if Thomas would confirm the opinion of the ballistics experts.

'I don't think so. The first killing convinces me. In competition you are allowed two unscored sighting shots . . . I think that's exactly what he did, took sighting shots.'

'What particular problems would he be up against, firing at, say, 800 yards or more?'

'Assuming he had accurate equipment his biggest problem would be to judge wind change. Remember that wind speed and direction will not be constant over the full length of the bullet's travel and the best judges in the business cannot guarantee not to make an error, human beings are just not sufficiently sensitive wind meters. To give you an example, the diameter of the Bisley bull ring in 1974 was 24 inches at 1,000 yards. If there were a gentle cross wind, enough to move a flag perceptibly away from the flagpole, a top marksman, after his sighting shots, would expect to put only seven out of ten shots into the bull.'

'That still sounds pretty good shooting to me.'

'Indeed it is. Especially when you know that a slight wind like that would deflect the bullet as much as 40 inches over 1,000 yards. No doubt you can see now why shooting over a distance of 1,000 yards or more is confined to target enthusiasts.'

'I have no reason to believe,' Leo said grimly, 'that the killer is anything but an enthusiast for his chosen sport.'

'Do you know what sort of rifle he has?' Thomas asked.

'Perhaps an army issue sniper's rifle,' Leo answered.

'Good enough,' Thomas confirmed. 'He's shooting at less than 1,000 yards so he wouldn't actually need a match rifle, a target rifle would do.'

'An army issue sniper's rifle would be a target rifle, would it?'

'As near as makes no difference, I imagine. I have a target rifle, would you like to see it?'

'If it's not too much trouble . . .'

'Not at all.'

Major Thomas left the room and Leo sipped carefully at his drink. He was acquiring a mass of background information but was unsure how much of it would be of real value to him. Yet he had learned that no information in a murder enquiry is ever useless and the time might come when he would be glad of Owen's readiness to answer his questions. 'Know your enemy' was no bad slogan for a detective.

'Here we are . . .' Owen placed the rifle in Leo's hands. It was solidly built, heavy, the bolt action making it look somewhat old-fashioned, the attached scopesight seeming an anachronism. The weapon was a delight to touch, had been lovingly cleaned and oiled, and Leo began to sense the reason for the devotion it so evidently inspired in its owner.

'So our man will probably have a rifle similar to this?' Leo asked.

'I'd say so. It's been rebarrelled to take the 7.62 military cartridge and it has an action built on the Mauser military one. Basically though it's the old Enfield No. 4 military rifle but it was modified for me by Fultons, the gunsmiths. Ever done any shooting yourself?'

'Yes. Not with a weapon quite like this though.'

'I don't shoot nowadays. I'm getting rather past it. Comes to us all.'

'This scopesight,' Leo said, 'he'd have one like this?'

'Probably. That's an X2. Doubt if you'd need greater magnification than that under 1,000 yards. I think the army go for an X6 though.'

Leo handed the rifle back to its owner. 'It's fairly heavy,' he commented. 'He must be fit to carry that about with him across country.'

'I don't know, you get used to it. As in all sports, you tone up the muscles by use,' Owen said, leaning forward in his chair to throw another log on the fire. 'Of course,' he added, returning to his drink, 'you will have gathered from all I've said that the murderer almost certainly has a practice range somewhere, or did have.'

'No, I hadn't thought that far ahead,' Leo admitted. 'What makes you think that?'

'I assume he stole the rifle and scopesight?'

'Yes, that's pretty certain.'

'He's made three first-class shots. He couldn't have done that without practice, without familiarizing himself with the equipment, perhaps even modifying it to suit his own build and personal preference.'

Leo made a mental note that Thomas mentioned only three shots. Unless he was a consummate actor he had no knowledge of the attempt on Bob Staunton.

'What kind of area would he need to set up a practice range?' he asked.

'Somewhere isolated, obviously. Ideal spot would be level ground facing a cliff. He could set up his target against the cliff and pace out his distances. There'd be no problem finding a hundred places like that anywhere in these hills.'

'You think he's living up in the hills then?'

'That would be my guess.'

'Living rough in a tent, say?'

'He'll not be living too rough. I don't suppose he'd be bothered for himself, but if he's really an enthusiast he won't risk his rifle. He'll have somewhere warm and dry, you can bet on that. I would if I were him.'

Leo, himself convinced of Thomas's innocence, hesitated before saying: 'You're not, I suppose?'

'Pardon?'

'You're not him?'

'Good Lord! . . . Ah, I see. I've had the training, suppose I've still got the skill. Fair comment, yes, fair comment.'

'Well?'

'Don't you think I'm a little old?'

'You look fit to me, Owen,' Leo said evenly.

'And I look like a murderer, do I?' said Owen, apparently amused rather than angered by Leo's casual half-accusation.

'In my experience murderers seldom look like murderers.'

'Really? How disappointing.'

'Even though you are no longer a member of a local rifle club, sooner or later the police will discover that you used to be, that you have this rifle here, that you are an expert shot. It might not be too much to suggest that you could be suspect.'

'I suppose not. Fascinating! Still, they can test fire my gun, check the rifling on the bullet with those fired by the murderer, can't they? I hope they do have some spent bullets for comparison?'

'I think so.'

'Oh well, that puts me in the clear then,' Owen said complacently. 'Care for another drink?'

Detective Chief Superintendent Staunton, considering that he had put in a good day's work and was entitled to his relaxation, settled in for a cheerful evening with Glynis and Alf King and the regulars of The Yellow Fox. Under the influence of good company and a number of glasses of Glenfiddich his headache disappeared and he felt none the worse for his narrow escape from death.

It was somewhat reluctantly that he made his way to the telephone in the kitchen when Chief Superintendent Davies rang shortly after 9 p.m.

'Has Bennett coughed up, Ewen?' he asked.

'I'm afraid not, Bob. Not only will he not say a word, he threatens to sue us for false arrest.'

'Oh yeah, worries me to death, that.'

'You know the lads found the bullet?'

'No. I left when they arrived at the caravan. Have you matched it?'

'Yes. Same rifle, boy. No doubt about it.'

'That's it then, we've just got to persuade young Jimmy to talk.'

'Yes . . . we don't have a shred of evidence against him of course . . .'

'Ewen, we'll have to go back to that caravan tomorrow and take it to pieces, do a real job on it, and that farmhouse. I'm sure there's somethin' there.'

'Look, Bob, I'm not a man to back down, see? But I've got Bennett in my cells, no evidence against him, and now we're proposing to demolish his home. I think we'd better have a meeting at my office in the morning and talk it over.'

'If you want. I suppose we've got men guarding the farm and the van?'

'Yes. Shall we say nine in the morning?'

'Fine.'

'Oh, one small thing . . .'

'Yeah?'

'I'm told we have a file on Bennett. It'll be in my office by the morning.'

'That'll please Leo,' Bob chuckled, 'especially if it's a con for violence, eh?'

'I'm glad somebody's going to be pleased,' Davies said mournfully.

'Cheer up Ewen,' Bob advised. 'It's all over bar the shouting.'

The killer laid out his remaining cartridges on a blanket on the floor, then counted them. There were just seven.

He picked them up one at a time and polished them carefully with a soft cloth until they shone. When these were used, the problem of acquiring more would arise. That would mean that he would have to leave Wales for a while; such ammunition was not easily obtainable. That might be no bad thing. Although he had seen little evidence of it, he knew that the hunt must be mounting in intensity. It might be no bad idea to retreat and regroup, leave the hunters to wear out their energy chasing shadows. Winter was coming on. Let them freeze up in these hills whilst he enjoyed some of the luxuries he had recently denied himself.

In fact there was little of what others would call luxury that he missed. He would improve his diet, perhaps allow himself a few pints of beer, and certainly he would go to the cinema. He had a passion for Western films and once, on a rare visit to London, he had spent two whole days travelling from one cinema to another, catching afternoon, evening and late-night performances, sating himself with secondhand gunplay, remaining undeterred even when the actors fired a dozen or more shots without reloading their six-shot revolvers. He had been born out of his time. He would have given those quick-draw merchants a run for their money. Yes, he would certainly go to the cinema.

His father used to take him to the cinema. Big Dave had been a loud, hard drinking, rough-house merchant, a man who could handle anything and anybody. But he had not been able to defy the brain tumour that felled him when the boy was at the highly impressionable age of seven.

'Never let the bastards grind you down, boy, see?' he had said. 'Smash 'em in the teeth first, let 'em know you're not to be messed about, boy, that's the way.' And that had been the only legacy the boy had had from his ignorant and naturally aggress-ive father, except for a genetic propensity for violence.

Free of her domineering husband, the boy's mother turned to drink and a succession of men. The boy was an impediment, often abused, often the butt of drunken jokes, often frightened, often totally neglected. It was unfortunate that he was physically small. At school he was known as the runt. His rejection by his mother became a poison eating at his reason, and over the years the necessity to prove to the world that he stood for something, that, despite appearances, he was the son of his father, became overpowering.

It had been a long time before he discovered his natural talent with a rifle. When he did, he also discovered a pride in himself and in his ability, a pride based on the certainty that no one would grind him down any more. With a gun in his hand he was invincible.

What would his father have thought, seeing him now? He was smackin' 'em in the teeth, wasn't he? Just like the old man had said. And he wasn't finished yet. He had plans.

He wrapped the cartridges in separate strips of clean cloth, putting aside dreams of the future. He would not leave until those seven cartridges had been fired.

There was yet some killing to do.

CHAPTER NINE

At nine o'clock the following morning Bob and Leo left their
cars in a public car park in Portmadoc and walked to the incident
room. As they walked Bob relayed the information Chief Superintendent Davies had given him the night before.

'I reckon Ewen is getting a bit windy about keeping Bennett,'
Bob said.

'One can hardly blame him. If the balloon goes up, he is the
chap who will be holding the string,' Leo pointed out.

'We can't let Bennett go,' Bob said doggedly. 'We've got to
break him somehow.'

'I agree.'

'Really? I thought you might want to stick by the book.'

'As you say, Bennett is all we have. If he was in the army,
perhaps his bank raiding friend was as well.'

'Anything is possible, my son. By the way, how's the girl-
friend?'

'Nerys? She's fine,' Leo replied absently.

Bob was about to make a joke at Leo's expense but changed
his mind and led the way into the small car park at the rear of the
National Insurance building and up the iron stairs that led to the
incident room.

They found Chief Superintendent Davies in his office, looking more than ever like a worried dormouse. He stood up as they entered and waved them to chairs.

'Hope you don't mind, Bob,' he said, 'but I've asked the Chief Constable if he'd sit in with us at this conference. I've explained the situation to him.'

'Matter for you, Ewen,' Bob said, 'but I intend to keep hold of Bennett even if I've got to lock him up in my room at The Yellow Fox.'

'There shouldn't be any need for that,' Chief Constable Alex MacCready said, entering the room in time to catch Bob Staunton's last remark.

The other officers stood but MacCready waved them back to their chairs. 'Carry on with the argument, pretend I'm not here. I'll tell you what I think later.'

'There are some further details I can give you about Bennett before we begin,' Davies said, opening a file on the desk in front of him. 'He spent three years in the army, was convicted of theft, served four months' imprisonment and was dismissed the service two years ago. He has one civilian conviction, eighteen months ago, for poaching. He was fined and his shotgun confiscated . . .'

'When did he join the local rifle club then?' Bob asked.

'Some years back, before he served in the army. He kept up his membership until he was thrown out, which was a few weeks after he came back here having been released from the army prison at Colchester.'

'Sorry, mate. Carry on . . .'

'Bennett is twenty-nine, divorced, his parents live locally but have had no contact with him for years. They disown him, black sheep of the family, see. Can't say I blame them. There is no record of his being employed in the last two years and he doesn't draw national assistance. We've seen his ex-wife but she's living with another chap and isn't interested, hasn't set eyes on him since he left the army. He had a gun licence but that was revoked when he was thrown out of the rifle club and then arrested on the poaching charge. And that's all we know about James Bennett. He refuses to talk. He's still in his cell playing at Al Capone, calling for his lawyer and threatening to sue us. As I see it, we don't have a shred of evidence to hold him.'

'How much did he have on him when we nicked him?' Bob asked.

Davies looked at the file. 'One hundred and fifty pounds, and forty-seven pence,' Davies answered.

'And how much is that bike of his worth?'

Davies shrugged. 'Several hundred pounds . . . but it might be on hire purchase.'

'Okay. Forget the bike. Where'd he get 150 quid from? How's he been livin' if he ain't worked for two years?'

'Well . . . that is fairly obvious . . .'

'Exactly. He's been thievin'.'

'But the money cannot be identified, Bob. We still have no evidence to tie him in with the bank raids let alone the murders.'

'We have, Ewen. It might be circumstantial, it might not be strong, but it's there. He's got cash on him he shouldn't have, he lied to everyone about where he got it, said he was workin' as a plasterer, right? When Leo and I went to see him, I got shot at by the same rifle used for our murders, right? He warned me off askin' questions and when we nicked him he tried to assault me . . . Okay, I don't want to charge him with that, do I? He came off worst, but why'd he do it? Then, when he's nicked, he won't answer questions about the bank jobs or the murders, why? If he was in the clear he'd be snowin' us under with alibis, wouldn't he? But what does he do? He don't do nothin', he don't say nothin', he just screams for a brief because he wants out of that cell. Now, if all that ain't enough to hold him for a day or two I don't know what is!'

'It's very thin,' Davies said, looking across at the Chief Constable.

'What do you want to do, Bob?' Alex MacCready asked.

'I want to hold Bennett at least until we've searched the farm thoroughly and taken his caravan to pieces.'

'That's another thing,' Davies said. 'Suppose we demolish his caravan, find nothing, then have to release him? He could make mincemeat out of us.'

'Bob?' Alex MacCready enquired.

'We ain't paid to sit on the fence,' Bob said. 'If we did that all the time we'd never nick anybody. Look, you know what it's like in a murder enquiry, you need that little bit of luck to start you off, right? So the Good Lord gave us a break, gave us Bennett, gave us an ace to play, right? Like it? So if we don't use the aces we're given we might as well pack in.'

MacCready looked across at Leo Wyndsor. 'Any comments, Leo?'

'Bennett is all we have, sir,' Leo said. 'We have already arrested him and detained him overnight. In all the circumstances it seems worth the risk of holding him a little longer.'

'How long would you want?' MacCready asked Bob.

'Three days, sir.'

The Chief Constable stood up and the others followed suit. 'You can hold him for two days on my authority, Ewen,' he said. 'You may also demolish his caravan if you deem it necessary. I shall be in my office if you need me.'

'Sorry about that, Ewen,' Bob said when MacCready had gone.

'Don't be sorry, boy. I want to hold Bennett as much as you, but if I'd done it without putting Alex MacCready in the picture, without giving him the chance to say no, then he'd have had my guts for garters, see?'

'Let's forget it then and get on with the job. How soon can you raise a search team?'

'Oh . . . we can have them there in under an hour.'

'Right. I'll join 'em. You coming?'

'Why not?'

'Before you go, sir,' Leo said, addressing Davies.

'Yes?'

'I spoke to Major Thomas last night, you remember he resigned from the local rifle club, he was on your list?'

'Oh, yes. And?'

'Interesting talk but nothing else. I suppose we should send a D.C. to take a formal statement from him though.'

'Right. I'll arrange that with Sergeant Richards.'

There was a sudden sharp knock on the door and at Davies' invitation Sergeant Richards entered holding a message form.

'Just talking about you, Gwyn,' Davies said. 'See Mr Wyndsor before he goes, there's a statement to be taken, he'll give you the name and address.'

'Right, sir. There's a message here I thought you'd want to see. It's a reply to your message to the Home Office requesting information from the army.'

Davies took it, read it through quickly, then handed it to Leo Wyndsor.

'We can apply for an interview with the O.C., Advanced Weapons Training Centre, Exeter. Whatever that might be.'

'I would make a small bet that Exeter is where the army trains its snipers,' Leo said.

'In which case it seems the army might have something to tell us after all,' Davies commented.

'I would like to go, sir,' Leo said to Bob.

'What for?' Bob countered. 'We can get an officer from Exeter to do it.'

'I suggest this interview might be delicate,' Leo said. 'The army will not be anxious to provide information about failed snipers, if that is what we are faced with here. Besides, it might be helpful for the interview to be conducted by an officer familiar with the enquiry.'

'I must say, Bob,' Davies put in, 'I'm inclined to agree with him.'

'Outvoted, aren't I?' Bob said. 'You push off on holiday, then. Leave me to get me hands dirty searchin' that stinkin' hole Bennett calls home . . . and don't disappear for a week, neither!'

'If I leave immediately I can be back by . . . late afternoon tomorrow.'

'Job'll more than likely be all over by then,' Bob said sourly.

'Only if you can find a way to make Bennett talk,' Leo said.

'I've got somethin' in mind for friend Bennett,' Bob promised.

Leo telephoned Exeter, made an appointment to see a Colonel

Gordon at 10 a.m. the next morning, then drove straight to Dhys-Gla. As he drove, he thought of something else he could do before he left.

He found Nerys alone in the kitchen, washing her hands in the sink. For once she was wearing a skirt and jumper and she had released her hair to let it fall about her shoulders. She was, Leo thought, eminently desirable. She looked across and smiled at him as he entered the room.

'No work today, then?' she asked.

'Nothing worth the mention,' Leo replied, moving behind her and putting his hands round her waist. 'You are very beautiful,' he said.

'No I'm not. Besides, you are always coming in unexpectedly and catching me in my old clothes.'

'I never notice what you are wearing. I just see you.'

'I don't believe a word of it.' She extricated herself from his arms and took a towel from a rail near the cooking stove to dry her hands.

'You will, one day.'

She smiled at him. 'I'm not a fool, Leo Wyndsor. Flattery comes as easily to you as swimming to a fish. It's just the way you are.'

'It wasn't flattery, Nerys. It was what I felt, it was entirely spontaneous.' Somewhat to his surprise, he realized that it was true.

'Perhaps.'

'Don't you think you are being unfair? If you think I'm just a silver-tongued philanderer how am I ever to convince you of anything?'

'You don't have to, dear.'

'I don't understand.'

'No, I don't suppose you do.'

'You obviously don't care. It doesn't matter to you what I think or what I feel . . . about you or anything else . . .'

Nerys replaced the towel on the rail and grinned impishly at him. 'Don't sulk. It doesn't suit you.'

'You are . . . infuriating!'

'Leo, you are obviously far too used to having women fall at your feet as soon as they look at you. That's not good for a man, it fattens his ego.'

'I'm not listening. I warn you, Nerys, I don't give up easily.'

'I hope not,' Nerys said, then added: 'Leo, I have work to do. Do you want a cup of tea or did you just come in here to pester me?'

'I came in here to pester you.'

'You did not.'

'Once I was here I did.'

'Leo . . .'

'But before that I came in here to ask you some questions.'

'Yes, of course. Reporters always ask questions, don't they?'

She was smiling at him, her head a little on one side, a slightly sad look on her face.

'I'm not a reporter, Nerys. I am a Detective Inspector in the London police.' He had not intended to say it, but now that he had, he was conscious of relief.

Nerys watched him, her face tense now. She said nothing, waiting for him to speak again. Leo looked away, uncertain of her reaction.

'I did not choose to lie to you, I had no option. I was sent here to Wales with a senior officer, Bob Staunton, to assist in the investigation into the murders. We were told not to reveal our identities. We work for the murder squad at New Scotland Yard.'

'Your name,' Nerys said. 'Is your name really Leo Wyndsor?'

'Yes, it is. The only lie I told was about my occupation.'

'You are not married?'

'Of course not. Do you see a ring on my hand?'

'Not all married men wear a ring. Since I knew you were not who you said you were . . .'

'You knew?'

Now it was Nerys' turn to look away. 'Yes, I knew,' she said.

'How?'

'You are not a very good liar, Leo, besides which my father saw a book in your room, a small notebook. It had a crest on it, the Metropolitan Police crest, so we knew.'

'You could have told me.'

'It was none of our business. We knew you must have a good reason for not telling us.'

'And you thought, because I lied to you about my job, you thought I might be married. Is that why you have been so distant with me?'

'Certainly not! It was ... it was because I hardly knew you.' She was laughing happily, then she was close to him, her arms round his neck, her lips soft and warm on his mouth and there was no reality outside that embrace. And the passion she aroused in him was something far removed from the lust that other women had engendered. There was not a mutual taking but a mutual giving, not a desire just of the body but also of the spirit. There was a passage of time that neither counted. When they moved apart, both were slightly breathless.

They sat down together at the kitchen table, staring at each other as if each were afraid the other was a dream. They felt no need to vocalize their feelings, there was a sense of tranquillity now, a sense of unity.

'What about those questions?' Nerys asked eventually, breaking the spell.

'Questions?'

'You were going to ask me some questions.'

'Was I? ... Oh, yes. I had quite forgotten.'

'Something to do with your work?'

'Yes.'

'Well then?'

'We must talk, Nerys.'

She covered his hand with hers. 'We have all the time in the world to talk, my love.'

'Yes. I suppose we have.'

'So what did you want to ask me?'

Leo took the map from his pocket and laid it out on the table. 'It somehow seems obscene to talk about it at the moment,' he said.

'As long as this man is loose, darling, people are in danger, you are in danger.'

'Yes, you are right. Other people far more than me. So, I want you to look at the area inside this ring, between Betws-y-coed, Blaenau Ffestiniog, Trawsfynydd, Bala and back to Betws-y-coed. The crosses mark the places where the murders have taken place. I think this man is living somewhere inside this circle.'

'But how can I help?'

'You know this area well, you must have ridden over most of it, I should think.'

'Yes. Every inch at one time or another.'

'This man is living out in the open somewhere . . . can you think where he might be?'

'You mean in a tent? He could be anywhere.'

'No. I think he's under some sort of permanent cover. A derelict cottage, a barn perhaps, something like that.'

'There are no derelict cottages or barns that I know of . . . there are very few buildings of any kind except . . . well, there are the slate mines of course, over towards Blaenau Ffestiniog.'

'He won't be anywhere near people.'

'I don't mean those near the town. Up in the hills, around here . . .' she pointed out the spot, '. . . only about six miles from this house, there is quite a large mine that has been closed down for eighty years or more.'

'Are there buildings still standing?'

'Yes. I don't think any of them have a roof left but most of the stone-built buildings at least have the outer walls standing.'

'It's rather near the road but it might be worth a look.'

'You don't intend to go up there alone?'

'I do. This is only a wild hunch. I cannot justify the cost of involving goodness knows how many officers in a thorough search. I shall just look around and if I come up with anything I will send for the U.S. cavalry.'

'Leo, are you insane? Suppose he *is* there . . .'

'It's a very small risk. The sort of risk I get paid to take.'

'Then I shall come with you.'

'You will not.'

'But you said there was no risk.'

'I am trained to look after myself, you are not. If I had you with me you would add to the risk. Anyway, I do not intend to go today, I have to leave for Exeter.'

'Exeter?'

'Yes. I cannot tell you why but I shall be in no danger whatsoever.'

'Why can't someone else go?'

'Would you really want someone else to do my job for me?'

'Yes . . . No . . . Oh, I don't know!'

Leo took her hand. 'Will you help me pack?' he asked.

Bob Staunton spent the whole day with the search team. They began with the farm, much to the disgust of the two elderly brothers who ran it, taking the farmhouse room by room, then moving on to the outhouses, barns, chicken runs, stables and even the pigsties. They found nothing.

By the time they had finished, in mid-afternoon, the farming brothers were apoplectic with rage and more than one of the searching officers was smelling less than sweet. It was half past three when they left the farm to turn their attention to the caravan, and Chief Superintendent Davies was beginning to get anxious.

'Hell, Bob,' he said. 'If we come up with nothing from this search we really are in trouble. At the very least we'll have to replace this decrepit old caravan with a new one and MacCready won't like that, I can promise you.'

'We won't have to, mate,' Bob promised. 'I've got a feelin' in me water it's goin' to be all right. Tell your boys to start by takin' off the roof.'

With a voice that was less than certain, Davies gave the order. After an unrewarding and often unpleasant search at the farm, the officers took out their frustration on the elderly caravan, setting to with axe, hammer and saw. But surprisingly the old caravan put up a stern resistance and by seven in the evening they had only managed to demolish the roof and one side. They stripped off every panel, smashed their way into every cavity, and still they found nothing.

As darkness fell they abandoned the search for the day. Chief

Superintendent Davies looked as if the end of the world had come.

'Cheer up, mate,' Bob said confidently. 'It's there, and we're goin' to find it.'

'What's there?' Davies asked gloomily.

'Whatever it is,' Bob said, 'we'll find it. There's another day tomorrow.'

A light drizzle began, adding to Davies' misery. 'We better find something,' he said, 'or I'll never be able to hold my head up at Round Table again.'

And that, Bob concluded to himself with a grin, was probably the greatest tragedy that Ewen Davies could imagine.

At about the time that the search of the caravan was being called off, Leo Wyndsor arrived in Exeter after an uneventful drive. He booked into a modest hotel near the city centre and telephoned Dhys-Gla.

Daffyd Johns answered the phone.

'Daffyd, this is Leo,' Leo said.

'Safe journey, then, boy?' Daffyd asked.

'Yes. Very boring. I am already looking forward to being back with you.'

Daffyd laughed. 'No doubt. Well, you don't want to talk to me, do you? I'll get Nerys.'

Before Leo could protest that he was quite happy to talk to him at length, Daffyd had put down the phone. Then there was the sound of running footsteps and Nerys' breathless voice.

'Leo . . . ?'

'Yes, dear.'

'Are you all right?'

'Yes, of course.'

'I thought, when Daffyd said it was you, I thought something must be wrong.'

'No, nothing at all.'

'Oh, I'm so glad. You have something you wanted to ask me?'

'No . . . I don't know really. I just wanted to talk to you.'

'That's nice. I'm glad you called.'

'But now I am talking to you, I really do not know what to say . . .'

'I can think of something . . .'

'Yes . . .?'

'No. You have to think of it for yourself.'

'Give me a clue.'

'Certainly not!'

They talked for a further half-hour. Later, Leo could not remember what they had said, only that, although apart, they had been together.

The killer eased himself into his sleeping bag and doused all the candles but one. By the light of this he switched on his transistor radio and tuned in to a local news programme.

He lay half listening, half dozing, until the newsreader's words suddenly took meaning for him.

'. . . the police will not say why the man is at Portmadoc Police Station, only that he is helping them with their enquiries into a serious crime. When asked if the man had been interviewed by Detective Chief Superintendent Davies, who is investigating the three recent shootings near Portmadoc, a police spokesman refused to confirm or deny that this was so. The man, who is thought to live locally, is thought to have been at Portmadoc Police Station for more than twelve hours. Chief Constable Alex MacCready was not available for comment . . . Following the recent interim budget, T.U.C. leaders . . .'

The killer leaned over and switched off the radio. He lay awake for a long while considering the information. The news media were always anxious to jump to conclusions. They could be quite wrong in the inference they drew. The police had not named the man or said why he had been held. Certainly if the police *did* think that the man they held could help them in their efforts to identify the killer they were totally mistaken. There was no one at all with sufficient information to identify him or his hideout. Of that he was sure.

Unless . . . unless the police had had the wit to see that they would never catch him by investigating the shootings and were approaching him from a different angle, starting from another point of attack . . . but even then, no one had known of his private campaign and certainly no one knew of this hideout.

Common sense dictated that he had nothing to fear. He doused the last candle and settled down into the sleeping bag, surrounded by sounds and smells familiar, an animal secure in his lair. He had nothing to fear.

Even so, it was a long time before sleep came.

CHAPTER TEN

Chief Superintendent Staunton arrived at the partly demolished caravan at 9 a.m. on the Saturday morning to find that Davies and his officers were hard at work, already having removed one of the end sections and being engaged in dismembering it.

When Davies saw Bob arrive he left the scene of the destruction and came across the clearing to meet him.

'Nothing,' he said mournfully. 'Nothing at all, boy.'

'Beautiful mornin' for it, Ewen,' Bob said cheerfully, ignoring the threatening clouds above.

'The press got on to it,' Davies informed him. 'It was on the local news last night.'

'What was, us goin' into the demolition business?'

'No. The fact we've got Bennett in custody.'

'They give his name?' Bob enquired.

'No.'

'Good. And they obviously haven't found us here . . .'

'Not yet . . .'

'Excellent,' Bob said rubbing his hands together. 'Any minit now one of your lads is goin' to jump in the air wavin' his arms about and all your worries'll be over.'

Davies smiled wanly. 'Bring your crystal ball, did you?' he enquired.

'Here, Ewen. You aren't on a diet, are you?' Bob said suddenly.

'Yes. Not that you'd think so to look at me . . .'

'That's it then. That's what's upsettin' you. Knock it off old mate, get some good grub inside you, that's the game.'

'I can't do that, Bob. Bad for the heart, see . . . so the doctor said.'

'Listen, mate. You don't want to listen to them doctors. What do they know, eh? You listen to them and you'd end up never eatin' nothin'. I'll bet Neville Chamberlain had a doctor like yours.'

'Chamberlain?'

'It's historical fact, mate. Listen, I'll tell you . . .'

Whilst Chief Superintendent Davies was treated to the historical proof for the deleterious effects of dieting, the work on the caravan continued apace. Despite Bob's confident prediction of early success it was a further hour before the rear wall of the caravan fell, ripping the old solid-fuel fire out of its seating as it went, and revealing a six-inch-deep cavity beneath the floor.

An excited officer waved Staunton and Davies across. When the senior officers clambered up on to the remains of the floor and looked down into the space at their feet they shared a grin of triumph.

The cache produced a sawn-off shotgun and cartridges, a loaded .38 automatic, two coshes, a flick-knife, two stocking masks and a holdall containing just over £8,000 in used notes.

'If I was a psychiatrist,' Bob said, 'I'd reckon this Bennett felt basically insecure, in need of protection from the world, know what I mean?'

Davies was not listening. 'Got the bastard,' he breathed.

'True,' Bob said, 'but it ain't him we want, is it?'

He left Davies to take possession of their find and wandered over to where the personal possessions taken from the caravan had been packed into large plastic bags. He rooted about amongst them, pulled out a shirt, removed one cufflink from the sleeve and slipped it into his pocket. He continued his search until he found a pair of sunglasses. He dropped them on the ground and trod on them, then placed the remains in his pocket.

When he rejoined the ecstatic Davies he had an innocent smile on his face and he was whistling loudly and out of tune.

Later that morning Bob Staunton and Ewen Davies interrogated Jimmy Bennett in the interview room at Portmadoc Police Station. Bennett was still resplendent in his black leathers. They said nothing to him when they first entered the room. Bob sat down at the table and stared at him with an amused smile. Surprise flickered across Bennett's face as he recognized Bob, but he said nothing. Davies opened the suitcase he was carrying and placed the shotgun and the other items found at the caravan on the table, then he sat down beside Bob Staunton and stared at Bennett. Bennett looked away.

After a moment Bob broke the silence. 'Any questions?' he asked.

'No,' Bennett replied.

'I'm Detective Chief Superintendent Staunton from Scotland Yard, the murder squad,' Bob said. 'You've seen me before, remember?'

'Didn't know who you were, did I?'

'Or you wouldn't have tried to put the frighteners on me that night when I left The Stag?'

Bennett shrugged.

'Or tried to assault me when I went to your caravan to interview you, eh?'

'You've got a bloody cheek!' Bennett flared. 'You could've crippled me for life, man.'

'Where you're goin', you wouldn't have missed nothin',' Bob said laconically.

'The last time I saw you,' Davies began, 'I questioned you about a number of bank raids and three murders that have taken place in this area recently. You refused to say anything.' He pointed to the items on the table. 'We searched your caravan this morning and found these under the floor. Is there anything you want to say now? Remember you have been cautioned that you need say nothing. Well?'

'Nothing to say.'

'I suppose you realize,' Bob said, 'that you ain't goin' nowhere . . . except inside for a long, long time?'

Bennett shrugged. 'So you say.'

'It's a promise.'

'I want my lawyer.'

'Okay, Jimmy. Give us his name and phone number then . . .'

Bennett hesitated.

'Only the big boys can afford to buy themselves a bent brief, Jimmy,' Bob said sadly. 'You've been watching too much TV. So let's forget all that cobblers and get down to business, shall we, eh?'

'You want me to make it easy for you, don't you, copper? Well you can stuff yourself. I'm saying nothing.'

Davies leaned forward. 'You are going to be charged anyway, Jimmy. All we want to know is the name of your accomplice,' he said.

'What accomplice?' Bennett asked. 'I've done nothing, see. You think I have, you prove it.'

Davies exchanged a look with Bob Staunton, then stood up and began to pack the shotgun and the other incriminating items back into the suitcase.

'You a poof, Jimmy?' Bob asked conversationally.

'Like hell!'

'Just wondered . . . just wondered why you're so keen to do bird for your mate. Do the same for you, would he?'

'What mate?' Bennett spat out. 'I told you, I don't know what you're talking about, see?'

'Yeah, you told us. Well, think about it Jimmy. It ain't just the bank jobs, it's the murders as well. You could go down for the lot.'

'Crap!' Bennett said.

Bob grinned. 'Have a think about it, son,' he suggested. 'The way things look right now, you may not come out of nick in time to get buried.'

134

Out in the corridor Chief Superintendent Davies set to worrying again. 'He's not going to talk you know, Bob.'

'He'll talk.'

'But when? Something young Wyndsor said the other day, about time. Time isn't with us, is it? We could have another murder on our hands before Bennett breaks.'

'You got any bright ideas, then?' Bob enquired.

'No. I wish I had.'

'I have.'

'What's that?'

'Psychology, mate. Take his stormtrooper gear off him and give him the roughest old set of clothes you can find. That'll help cut him down to size. Psychology, see?'

'Okay. Not a bad idea, that.'

'I've got another one.'

'Yes?'

'We go and have lunch.'

Leo Wyndsor arrived promptly at 10 a.m. at the Advanced Weapons Training Centre in Exeter for his interview with Colonel Gordon. The building turned out to be a disused hospital on the outskirts of the city and the security, although little in evidence, was in fact very tight. At the front gate he was stopped and, when he had shown his warrant card, escorted to the main building by a substantially built young man who looked painfully out of place in civilian clothes.

The office into which he was shown was spartan and cold. On the single plain desk was a name card which said 'Colonel T. E. Gordon'. The escort offered Leo a chair.

'If you wouldn't mind waiting, sir. Colonel Gordon will be with you in a few minutes,' he said, then left Leo alone.

It was fully a quarter of an hour before Colonel Gordon put in an appearance and when he did he was profuse in his apologies. 'Terribly sorry to keep you waiting, old chap . . . had to take a class . . . care for a cup of tea?'

'Thank you, no.'

Gordon dropped the thick bundle of files he had brought

135

with him on to the desk and took his seat. He was a wiry, hard-looking man, apparently in his early forties, dressed as if for a day's rough walking. He smiled pleasantly at his visitor as he opened the top file and flicked over a couple of typed sheets.

'Very well then, Inspector Wyndsor, how can I help you?' he asked.

'Exactly in the way your file indicates, Colonel. I imagine you have been authorized to give the information requested?'

'More or less. However, I have not been told exactly what information you require, only that I am to co-operate so far as security permits.'

'Then there should be no problem,' Leo said. 'As a police officer I am bound by the Official Secrets Act and I doubt if my security rating is lower than any member of your staff here. After all, were that not so, I would hardly have been permitted this interview.'

'Quite so, quite so,' said Gordon hastily, 'I was simply quoting from my instructions. Now, perhaps you could explain the circumstances and tell me what I can do to help?'

'No doubt you will have read in the national press that there have been three murders recently in North Wales?'

'Yes, of course . . .'

'The circumstances of these murders are such that we have reason to believe that they were committed by a man who is not only an expert shot but who has had specialized training, the kind of training you give here. Also, the indiscriminate selection of victims suggests that the man is killing for the sake of it, for the love of it if you will, that he is mentally unstable. If you read the newspaper reports perhaps you came to similar conclusions yourself . . .'

'I had not given it thought, actually, but your deductions do seem logical, I must say.'

'Since it was the army authorities who directed me here and arranged this interview, I am left to conclude that if we are right, if our man was trained as a sniper, he was in fact trained at this establishment.'

'That might well be the case,' Gordon said guardedly, 'if you are right.'

'Very well, then. First of all I must ask for details of any man who has passed through your course in the last, say, five years and subsequently been found to be temperamentally unsuited to the work, perhaps even dismissed the service due to some psychological impediment.'

Colonel Gordon closed the file slowly, then sat back in his chair, clearly selecting his words with care. 'You must understand, we draw men for this course almost exclusively from the Royal Marines, who are in any event a select force, and we only take the best. Once selected for the course they are screened, and this screening includes psychological tests. Their performance is monitored throughout the course and our standards are very high. It would not be especially unusual for a complete intake to fail, we can afford no errors. So you see, the chances that your man was a fully trained sniper are remote.'

'I deal all too often in remote chances,' Leo said.

Gordon scratched thoughtfully at his chin. 'However ... I will see what I can do. I have only been here for a year myself but if such a man was failed during a course the records should still be available to me. If he was posted to a unit and subsequently dismissed, well, that would take longer to discover.'

'I quite understand.' What Leo understood was that Gordon had someone in mind but was as yet not prepared to commit himself. For a trained sniper to be dismissed the service would be so unusual that the news would have certainly reached someone in Gordon's position. Indeed, it probably would have resulted in high-level consternation and a review of the screening for would-be recruits.

'Was there anything else?' Gordon asked.

'Yes. The killer has possession of a rather special rifle, a target rifle our ballistics experts suggest, and ammunition to match. Not the sort of weapon readily available to a thief, and almost certainly he stole it. I have to ask if the army is missing such a weapon or ammunition.'

Gordon was looking distinctly unhappy. 'It could have been a privately owned rifle, a member of a rifle club . . .'

'I'm afraid not. We have checked. Incidentally, the ammunition he is using is F.N. manufacture, 7.62 mm.'

'Yes . . . well . . . I'll have to check on that.'

Leo was beginning to feel rather sorry for Gordon. Clearly this murder investigation was rattling some skeletons in the army cupboard. On the other hand, what had begun as a rather speculative enquiry was now beginning to look promising.

'If there had been such a theft it would, I imagine, have been investigated internally, by the S.I.B.,' Leo said conversationally, 'so there would be a record of the investigations on file.'

'Oh, yes. I trust that is all?'

'Almost. If we are indeed hunting one of your snipers it would be a great help to know the extent of his training, so that we know what we are up against. Perhaps whilst I am here I could be shown round, see some of your chaps in training?'

On this point Gordon was adamant. 'I'm afraid not. That I cannot arrange.'

'It might possibly save a life.'

'Even so. Look, we once had to arrange for a TV documentary crew to film here, political pressure applied I imagine, took us weeks to arrange things so that they did not show anything damaging. It would be a major disruption of the whole course to arrange for you to be shown round . . . I'm sure you understand.'

'Not exactly. Surely my security rating is higher than a TV documentary crew? My interest is not personal and what I see would not be for publication.'

'I understand that . . .'

'Well, then . . .'

Gordon hesitated. 'Inspector, this much I can tell you. Not all the men on our courses are army personnel, some are . . . some are from elsewhere and I have no authority to permit anyone, and I mean anyone, to so much as catch sight of them.'

'And they cannot be separated from the rest of the course?'

'Not without a massive disruption of training, I'm sorry.'

Leo recognized a blank wall when he saw it. He had a fair idea who the mysterious civilians would be and knew he would get no thanks for pressing the matter.

'Very well, Colonel,' he said. 'I shall not pursue that request. As for the rest . . .?'

Colonel Gordon looked considerably relieved. 'If you would bear with me whilst I make a couple of telephone calls?' he said.

'By all means,' Leo replied.

Gordon was absent for nearly half an hour. When he returned he looked rather more at ease, as if some weight had been removed from his shoulders.

He smiled at Leo as he resumed his seat and said: 'Sorry to be so long. Fortunately for both of us I have been able to secure certain permissions regarding the information you asked for . . .' He selected a file, removed several typed sheets of headed paper neatly stapled together and handed them over. 'This is a copy of an S.I.B. report which you can peruse at your leisure. As you will see, about a year ago we had a modified bolt action sniper's rifle with telescopic sight and about forty rounds of sniper ammunition stolen.'

Leo scanned the report. As he did so he asked: 'Does sniper ammunition differ from other types?'

'Only in as much as it is graded and checked to eliminate, or at least minimize, misfires.'

'I see there was no break-in effected . . . one is left to assume that the thief was familiar with the premises here.'

'I think you will see that the investigating officer came to the same conclusion.'

Leo folded the copy report and put it in his pocket. 'Which brings us to the second part of my enquiry . . .'

'I think we can help you there . . . but not today. As I said earlier, if you remember, I have only been here a year. The chap you really want to speak to is now on active duty but if you give me a telephone number I'll arrange for him to contact you.'

'Such a man as I described does exist then,' Leo said, writing out the telephone number at Dhys-Gla and handing it over. '. . . a sniper discharged as being psychologically unfit?'

'Something like that, I gather,' Gordon said guardedly.

'When he telephones me at that number, ask him to refer to me by name, not rank, if you would,' Leo said.

Gordon grinned. 'I understand.'

'Can I know the name of the officer who will contact me?'

'I don't think his name is important. I promise you he will call as soon as possible ... and I think you will find what he has to say will be of interest.'

Leo made a gesture of acceptance. 'I am very grateful for all your help, Colonel Gordon,' Leo said. 'There is one last thing. We really have no idea of what we are up against. Since I cannot see your men training for myself, can you tell me what sort of capabilities this man would have, without prejudicing security, of course?'

Gordon sat back in his chair and pulled thoughtfully at his ear. 'Well ... if he is a trained sniper I should advise your chaps to be very careful how they approach him. He could probably put a bullet into any reasonable target, given fair conditions, at anything up to 1,000 metres and he would be trained only to make a killing shot. He'd be a damned dangerous chap to go after up in those mountains, even if he were sane.'

'We had already concluded that he is an expert shot ...'

'He would be ... although being a super shot is not the only or even perhaps the main prerequisite of a sniper. They are trained in fieldcraft for instance, and we expect them to close to within 180 to 200 metres of a target unseen. Certainly at that range we would expect him to achieve near perfection but at 1,000 metres we would settle for him being simply expert. To give you some idea of his fieldcraft capabilities, on the final test of our course the men are allowed to camouflage themselves and are then given two minutes to disappear in an open field. Trained spotters with the advantage of height look for them and direct men with radios to find them. If they are found they have failed the course. It's that tough.'

'I'm beginning to be sorry I asked,' Leo said. 'Anything else you can tell me?'

'He will be expert at map reading. Our chaps must be able to spot a target on the ground, spot it on an aerial photo, and plot it on a map. He will also be a trained observer and have damned good eyesight. He's likely to see you long before you see him.'

'You make your chaps sound like supermen,' Leo commented.

'No, not supermen. In fact the best snipers are average height, average build, nothing special to look at, average in most ways except for the special talents we encourage here. But they are an *élite*, the course is less rigid and formal than others, we encourage individuality, and there are fewer restraints as to dress, for example. Don't misunderstand me, a man who passes this course *is* special, we like to say that he is the ultimate infantryman.'

'You mentioned dress,' Leo said. 'What manner of dress would our man be likely to adopt?'

'Well, if he were copying our chaps he would have camouflaged trousers and a jacket with a hood, dark-coloured balaclava helmet and deliberately dulled boots. He would wear no badges of rank or other metal objects which might reflect light, his face would be daubed and all his clothing, including the helmet, would be strung with strips of camouflage cloth. The rifle and scopesight would be bound with camouflage cloth and hung with strips. That's assuming he was preparing for active duty.'

'I think this chap is on permanent active duty,' said Leo grimly.

'There is one thing,' Gordon said. 'I suppose it *is* only one chap you're looking for?'

'We have assumed so.'

'I wondered because in fact our chaps usually work in pairs, one to make the shot, the other to spot for him.'

Which thought did nothing for Leo's peace of mind as he drove back to North Wales.

At two o'clock in the afternoon Bob Staunton went alone into the interview room at Portmadoc Police Station and confronted Jimmy Bennett, now dressed in ill-fitting jacket and trousers and a frayed open-necked shirt. Bennett was far from happy.

'They took my clothes,' he complained.

'Forensic tests,' Bob said blandly, taking a seat at the bare table.

'I'll complain to my M.P., see,' Bennett threatened.

'Know who he is?' Bob asked.

'No. But I'll find out . . .'

'Let me know when you do, I'll pass on the message for you.'

'What d'you want anyway?' Bennett asked truculently.

'Goin' to tell you somethin',' Bob said.

'More crap!' Bennett prophesied.

Bob leant his head forward and pointed to the scar where the bullet had creased him. 'See that?' he asked.

Bennett said nothing.

'Bullet did that,' Bob told him.

'So?'

'When I was waiting for you at your caravan yesterday, someone took a pot shot at me with a rifle.'

'It wasn't me,' Bennett said quickly.

'Could have been.'

'You didn't find a rifle at the caravan, did you?'

'No. You had time to get rid of it, didn't you mate?'

'It wasn't me!'

'You was in a rifle club Jimmy, until you got kicked out. You know how to use a rifle, don't you, mate?'

'It wasn't bloody me!'

'As it happens,' Bob said, 'I believe you. I'm just pointin' out that we could make a good case against you. Matter of fact, I think it was your mate.'

'I'm saying nothing, see,' Bennett said. But he was less certain now.

'So I got to thinkin',' Bob continued. 'Nobody knew I was goin' to be at your caravan yesterday, right? Nobody. So whoever it was shot at me, he weren't there lookin' for me, was he? He was there lookin' for someone else and I just got in the way . . .'

Bob let that sink in before he continued.

'I reckon your mate's decided you're a liability, Jimmy. You're too flash, too obvious. You're a bloody danger to him, mate. He's after puttin' you out of the way.'

142

'Crap,' Bennett said, but with less conviction than before.

'I ain't finished yet,' Bob said. 'It so happens we found the bullet your mate fired at me. That bullet, my son, matches the bullets used to kill the three people he's used as target practice up in the mountains. How about that then, Jimmy boy?'

Bennett said nothing but his eyes were glazed with extreme concentration. Bob let him work at it for a moment before speaking again.

'Let me spell it out for you Jimmy,' Bob said. 'You and your mate have knocked over three banks in the last year. Two people got killed, right? I'll bet it was your mate what killed both of 'em. There weren't no need for it, he's a nutter, right? Makes no difference, you was with him so that puts you in for murder anyway. But, unbeknown to you, he's been doing a bit of rifle practice up in the mountains, killed three more people, and when he thinks things might be gettin' a bit hot, he has a go for you. Nice bloke, eh? Nice mate to have, that.'

Bennett had gone pale. He was clasping his hands together to stop them shaking. All the arrogance had drained away from him.

'All of which is fine, Jimmy lad,' Bob said thoughtfully, 'but it leaves me with a problem, don't it?'

'Eh?' Bennett had not been listening.

'I said I've got a problem. I'm expected to catch murderers, right? That's what I get paid for. I've got to produce results, right? You won't tell me who your mate is, so I can't get him, can I? That bein' so, Jimmy, I've got to make the best of what I've got, haven't I?'

'What d'you mean, then?'

'You're all I've got Jimmy, so you've got to take the lot. Three bank jobs, includin' them two murders, then the other three murders. All down to you, Jimmy.'

'You can't do that! You ain't got no proof!'

Bob sighed. 'Watch me,' he said.

He took from his pocket the single cufflink and the broken sunglasses he had taken from the caravan and laid them on the table.

'Recognize them?' he asked.

Bennett stared but said nothing.

'Don't matter. They're covered with your prints. Now this,' Bob said, pointing at the cufflink, 'I found at the scene of the murder of Nurse James . . . and those,' pointing at the broken sunglasses, '. . . I found at the scene of the murder of a bloke called John Williams. Now what we got here is . . .'

'It's a bloody set-up!' Bennett shouted.

'Yeah,' Bob agreed, 's'pose it is.'

He collected the items and put them back in his pocket. Bennett watched him with sick fascination.

'I give beautiful evidence,' Bob confided. 'Juries take one look at me and fall over themselves to convict me prisoners. It's practice, see. Spent a lot of time in the witness box, I have . . .'

'You bastard . . .' Bennett said slowly.

Bob smiled as he got up and walked to the door. 'See you in court, Jimmy,' he said.

Chief Superintendent Davies was waiting outside the door. 'What did you say to him, Bob?' he asked.

'Not a lot, Ewen,' Bob said. 'Just quietly pointed out the error of his ways, explained some of the advantages of truth and honesty, you know . . .'

'I don't believe you . . .'

'He did,' Bob said complacently.

Leo Wyndsor arrived back at the incident room at Portmadoc shortly after 5 p.m. and found Bob Staunton and Ewen Davies in the latter's office.

'Got it solved, have you?' Bob enquired.

'Not exactly, sir, but I have obtained some very detailed and useful information on snipers and their capabilities.'

'Oh well, worth the trip, that,' Bob said sarcastically.

'It was,' Leo replied. 'I'll make the information up in note form and have it copied for you.'

'You should join the Civil Service,' Bob suggested, 'they like paperwork and all, I'm told. That all you got?'

'No. About a year ago a sniper's rifle and ammunition were

stolen from the Advanced Weapons Training Centre at Exeter. No one has ever been arrested and the rifle and ammunition are still missing.'

'That's more like it,' Bob said. 'Any suspects?'

'No, but it had to be someone with knowledge of the Centre. It lends credence to my theory that the killer is a trained sniper. Colonel Gordon is making enquiries to identify any trained sniper dismissed the service in the last five years as psychologically unsuitable. I think he's got someone in mind actually, he is arranging for another officer to telephone me. I gave the number at the farm where I am lodging.'

'Who is this other officer, Leo?' Davies asked.

'Gordon would not give me the name. It's all frightfully hush-hush. Apparently the chap is on active service somewhere, which suggests that the dismissed sniper had passed through the course and had been posted to an active service unit himself.'

'Any reason why this sniper of yours shouldn't be Jimmy Bennett's mate?' Bob enquired.

'None at all that I know of,' Leo replied. 'I am desperately hoping that's who it will turn out to be. Has Bennett talked yet?'

'Not yet, mate. But I've given him some medicine to loosen his tongue.'

'One other thing Colonel Gordon mentioned in passing. The snipers he trains usually work in pairs. One spotting targets and the other actually doing the shooting.'

'I thought snipers worked on their own,' Bob said.

'So did I. And I am still convinced that our killer is working alone.'

'I suppose Bennett could have been spotting for his mate,' Davies suggested.

Bob shook his head. 'Jimmy is a know-nothing yob,' he asserted, 'he'll go along with his mate knockin' off a bank clerk on a blaggin' job because there's loot in it, but he ain't a ravin' nutter. I don't reckon he knows anything about what his mate's been up to on the side. What time is this bloke going to ring you, Leo?'

'I don't know exactly. Fairly soon, I imagine.'

'Better get back to your farm and hold the girl-friend's hand then, hadn't you? We don't want her dad takin' strange phone calls from army officers, do we?'

'Will you be here, sir?'

'No, mate. I'm goin' back to The Yellow Fox for a decent meal and a noggin. Give me a ring if anything happens here, Ewen.'

'I'll do that, Bob.'

'And you, Leo, if that bloke rings.'

'Yes, sir.'

'And Leo . . .'

'Yes, sir?'

'Wipe the lipstick off your shirt collar.'

He and Davies shared a grin but Leo was having none of that.

'This shirt was clean on this morning,' he said. 'Getting back to business for a moment, what happens if, despite your medicine, Bennett still refuses to name his accomplice?'

'Then we've got to find some other way of findin' out who he is and where he is, ain't we?'

'Bennett has no known associates who are likely suspects or Mr Davies would have come up with them by now. So how do we go about identifying his partner and tracing him?'

'Got any ideas?' Bob asked.

'I'm afraid not,' Leo admitted.

'Then think about it,' Bob suggested.

Leo did think about it on the drive to Dhys-Gla. There were, as he saw it, three possibilities: either the killer was indeed Jimmy Bennett's partner in crime, or if the two were not the same man, it was the suspect ex-sniper or, and Leo had no wish to believe this, the killer was still a totally unknown quantity.

Yet, even if the last were the case, there was a faint ray of hope. The killer was living semi-rough up in the mountains, of that Leo was sure. That being so, it was at least theoretically possible to discover his hideout. Leo decided not to wait and see if Bob's medicine worked on Bennett; it just might not.

When Leo arrived back at Dhys-Gla Nerys was waiting for him at the front door. She kissed him, then took his arm and led him into the house.

146

'I was just beginning to get worried,' she said.

'Why?'

'I worked out what time you might be back and I thought it would probably be about five o'clock.'

'I had a call to make in Portmadoc.'

'Business?'

'Of course.'

'That's all right then ... Leo ... I told the others you had gone to Exeter. I had to tell them something, you don't mind, do you?'

'Not at all.'

'They are in the kitchen, waiting to say hello.'

Leo dropped his overnight case in the hall and followed Nerys into the kitchen.

Daffyd clasped his hand. 'Thank God you're back safe and sound,' he said.

Leo grinned. 'I wasn't exactly going to war,' he protested gently.

'You never know, boy, you never know,' said young Jones enigmatically.

'I went there once,' said Morwenna.

'To Exeter?' Leo asked politely, presuming that was what Morwenna meant.

'No, Torquay. We went to Torquay on holiday. That's near Exeter, isn't it then?'

'Well, not far away.'

'They had palm trees at Torquay,' Morwenna said. 'I remember they had palm trees ...'

'Don't talk wet, girl,' said young Jones. 'Palm trees is in Africa.'

'And in Torquay ...'

Leo shared a smile with Daffyd and Nerys and wisely stayed out of the argument. Having shown his face, Leo left them in the throes of preparing the evening meal and took his overnight bag up to his bedroom. He washed and changed and came back downstairs to the sitting-room to await the call to dinner.

After a few minutes Nerys came in. She was wearing a simple

pale green dress which set off her hair and clung entrancingly to her body.

'You look good enough to eat,' Leo said.

Nerys blushed and smoothed down her already unwrinkled dress in an unconsciously nervous gesture. 'Are you staying in tonight?' she asked.

'Yes, if you come and sit on my knee.'

'Someone might come in,' she protested.

'Then they'll see no more than they expect,' Leo said.

'Perhaps, but none the less I'll sit over here,' she said, taking a chair opposite him. 'If I get too close to you I can't think straight.'

'Why do you want to think straight?'

'Because I do.'

'That's no answer.'

'It's my answer. Did you see any pretty girls in Exeter?'

'Not that I noticed. I was in too much of a hurry to get back here to see you.'

'You're only saying that because you think it's what I want to hear.'

'It happens to be the truth. And it *was* what you wanted to hear, wasn't it?'

'Yes. But that's beside the point ... what are you doing tomorrow?'

'Getting up very early.'

'What do you call very early?'

'Five. I shall leave the house at six.'

'Why?'

'I intend to visit that old mine working you told me about. I'll take Red if you have no objections, it will be easier on horseback.'

'You're going looking for this murderer,' she said flatly.

'No. I am looking for his hideout.'

'Do you have to?' Nerys asked quietly.

'Yes, I have to.'

'I suppose ...' Nerys said slowly, '... I suppose you are dedicated to your job, you would never want to do anything else, would you?'

148

'I am far from dedicated to my job,' Leo said. 'In fact there are times when I positively detest the work. Unfortunately I have never found anything else that I would be qualified for and which would suit me.'

'But one day you might?'

'One day I might.'

Nerys stood up and offered him her hand. 'I think I heard Morwenna calling us for dinner,' she said.

After the meal the whole family adjourned to the sitting-room and the conversation became general. At ten o'clock Nerys excused herself and went to bed, soon followed by Morwenna and young Jones, leaving Leo and Daffyd Johns alone to finish the last few drops of blackberry wine in an otherwise dead bottle.

The silence between them was warm and companionable. Daffyd drained the bottle into the glasses and sat back comfortably in his chair. Leo twirled his glass in his fingers, watching the play of light in the dull red liquid.

Eventually he asked: 'Daffyd, is Nerys very like her mother?'

'Yes, very like her,' Daffyd answered. 'My wife was killed in a car accident when Nerys was nine years old, you know.'

'I'm sorry, I had no idea . . .'

Daffyd waved the apology aside. 'We were very close. I miss her still. Her death was pointless, heartbreaking. In all her life she had done nothing but good, so I asked God why, why he took her from me. I had a crisis of faith. It seemed a brutal, evil thing for him to permit. She had gone and I was left only with her body, her discarded flesh and bones to bury, she had gone . . .'

'Then how did you . . . how could you come to terms with her death?' Leo asked.

'Eventually I understood that she had died from random chance, as a result of the free choice God has to give us if we are not to be simply angelic robots. God had no part in her death. He felt my pain and shared it. I realized that my suffering was selfish. Her death meant that she was with the Lord. How could I regret that? My regret was for myself, that she was no longer with me.'

It was a moment before Leo spoke. Then he said: 'Thank you,

Daffyd . . . thank you for telling me. I think I can understand something of how you felt when you lost her.'

'Perhaps you can, Leo,' Daffyd said. 'Perhaps you can.'

'Did Nerys . . . did she tell you what my job really is?'

'She did . . . but your secret is safe with us.'

'I'm sure it is. Daffyd . . . when this job is over I will have to return to London but I would like to come back, for a holiday. Would you mind?'

Daffyd smiled. 'We would all be delighted,' he said.

Leo finished his drink, put down his glass and stood to leave. 'Then that is settled,' he said. 'Thank you, Daffyd. Well, I have an early start in the morning . . .'

Daffyd took Leo's arm as they walked out into the hall. 'Goodnight, Leo,' he said. 'God bless.'

Bob Staunton woke suddenly just after seven the following morning to be greeted by the remarkable sight of the gigantic Alf King dressed only in a pair of pink and green striped pyjamas, bending over him and shaking him by the shoulder.

' *'Ere*, wake up Bob, there's a geezer on the dog and bone wants yer.'

'Eh?' Bob grunted, struggling to come awake.

'Bloke on the phone, says 'is name's Davies, says it's urgent. Bloody wants to be, I says, this time in the bloody mornin'!'

Bob scrambled out of bed. 'Sorry, Alf. Somethin' must've come up. Go back to bed, if I've got to go out I'll creep out quiet like.'

'Nah,' Alf said, scratching the exposed hairs on his chest. 'I'll get the missus up and started on the breakfast, might as well.'

Bob hurried down to the kitchen of The Yellow Fox, still only half awake, blinking his eyes to clear his vision and holding on to the walls as he went down the stairs as an aid to uncertain balance.

'Yeah?' he enquired into the receiver.

'Ewen Davies, Bob.'

'What's up, couldn't you sleep?'

'It's Jimmy Bennett . . . he wants to see you. He won't talk to anyone else, only you. I think your medicine worked . . .'

CHAPTER ELEVEN

Leo Wyndsor was awake long before Bob Staunton that Sunday morning. The diminutive travelling alarm clock was on the bedside table, no more than a foot away from his head. When it erupted noisily at five-thirty he was jerked into sudden awareness of the bitter cold and solid blackness of the room and for a sudden horrifying moment as his brain struggled to orientate itself it was as if he had woken in his tomb.

He switched on the bedside lamp and allowed himself a minute beneath the sheets to recover before hastily throwing on his dressing-gown, donning his slippers and fumbling his way down the landing to the bathroom. By the time he had washed, shaved and dressed himself he had begun to feel somewhat more human but he still felt heavy from lack of sleep and his movements were slow and carefully calculated.

As he reached the top of the stairs he was aware of fresh cooking smells from the kitchen. He found Nerys still dressed in her nightclothes but her hair carefully combed, cooking breakfast for him.

'Nerys ... what are you doing?' he asked, querying the obvious.

'You can't go out at this time of the morning without food, now can you?' she replied defensively.

'I certainly intended to.'

151

'I know. That's why I came down. Take a seat, it's nearly ready.'

Instead of which Leo came up behind her and cuddled her to him. She prudently removed the frying pan from the heat before turning in his arms and holding him tightly. He was vitally aware of her warmth, her softness and of the heady scent of her. As he kissed her his hand moved up to cover her breast. She let it remain there for a moment before gently removing it.

'Do you not want me to touch you?' Leo asked.

'Yes . . . of course I do. I could easily become addicted to it.'

'Then why did you stop me?'

'Because I like it.'

Leo kissed her eyes. 'I can hardly seduce you here in the kitchen, can I?'

'I don't want you to seduce me anywhere, not yet. No, that's not true, I desperately want you to make love with me, my whole body aches for you sometimes but . . .'

'But what?'

'I don't have much to offer, but I can at least go to my marriage bed as a virgin. I have waited so long, I think I can wait a little longer, if you will help me.'

Leo kissed her nose and her mouth. 'Then we had better have a very short engagement and a very long honeymoon,' he proposed.

The manner of the proposal did not offend Nerys. She had known Leo not just for a few days, but all her life. Their union was predestined, inevitable.

'Yes please,' she said. 'On a desert island where no one will disturb us and we can go naked all the time.'

'If we did that I would be making love to you all day and all night.'

She kissed him quickly before turning out of his arms. 'Promises, promises . . .' she teased. 'Better sit down and eat before you promise something else you can't deliver.'

'I will remind you of that . . . later,' Leo threatened, grinning. 'I'll stand for no excuses, no sudden headaches or three-week menstrual cycles or fits of tiredness.'

Nerys placed his breakfast on the table, led him to the chair and sat him in it. 'There will never be any lipstick on your collar except mine,' she said. 'By the time I've finished with you you won't have the energy even if you have the desire.'

'I've done my running around, Nerys.'

'I don't want to hear about that. Get on and eat or you will be late.'

Leo ate what he could whilst Nerys sat beside him, drinking tea and watching his face. Then it was time for him to go and the parting was painful, as if it were to be for ever. Nerys went with him to the stables.

'Do take care, my love,' she said, anxiously.

'I will,' Leo promised.

She must have been up very early for she had already saddled Red for him to ride. Red actually belonged to her father but Daffyd seldom rode these days so the horse had rather less exercise than he needed, especially of late, and was skittish and eager to be on his way. Nerys checked the tack yet again.

'You promise?'

'I promise.'

They kissed again before Leo climbed into the saddle. Nerys watched until Leo disappeared up the track towards the road, then went into the house locked herself in her bedroom and prayed for him. But even afterwards she was tense and nervous, beset by a powerful premonition of impending disaster.

She felt strangely incomplete in Leo's absence, as if some part of her had left with him. She knew then that it would be this way until the day they died. They would never again be apart, even when they were not physically in each other's presence.

It was comforting knowledge and she held it to her, taking inner warmth from it, hoping it was a shield.

It was barely dawn as Leo crossed the Penmachno road and took a track through the forest on the other side. After half a mile or so of steeply rising ground, the massed ranks of conifers stopped suddenly, in a near-straight line, as if in obedience to some immutable law that not one foot higher could they sustain themselves.

As the track emerged from the forest it climbed more steeply, passing by a series of huge, naked rock steps, some as much as twenty feet high, and on the ledge of each step was a thin covering of dark green moss and short grass beneath a scattering of deciduous trees which had shed leaves on the ground, mottled in brown and red in their dying. The trees clung limpet-like to the rock, roots delving down into cracks and crannies, grasping for moisture and nutrient. Beyond the steps, other trees had found a precarious home on the slopes of the mountain, but within 200 feet they too, shrinking in size with the slope, gave up the unequal struggle for survival.

The track petered out and now there was only the tough rye grass sharing place with dark mauve heather, hardy ferns and an occasional vivid green gorse bush dusted with yellow blooms. Here began the eruptions of granite and slate, dark grey outcrops of rock forcing their way through the thin, unfertile soil, a warning of harsher terrain to come.

Leo consulted the map that Nerys had marked for him. His way led round the side of the mountain, up into the high tablelands between the peaks where place-names were sparse but contour lines plentiful. The sky had been overcast, but now, as if to bestow a blessing on Leo's venture, a single patch of blue appeared and the sun was unexpectedly bright, its rays picking out the unclothed head of one distant peak, painting it yellow-white, making a contrast with the surrounding black-greens and tan-browns, creating instant beauty from the bleakness.

For a while there was still evidence of man's attempt to utilize the impoverished land. Low drystone walls high on the mountainside, built laboriously stone upon stone without benefit of binding material, marking out steeply sloped fields for no obvious purpose since there was a natural barrier of barren rock above the grass line. Yet man had to leave his mark, draw his puny straight lines where nature intended majestic irregularity, intent on duping himself that he was master here.

Leo followed one such wall to where a stone bridge with a low coping and a single central support spanned a shallow turbulent river, fed by a hundred small streams that were but tiny white scars on the faces of the surrounding mountains. The water was ice-cold, grey-green and flecked with white, foaming over brief falls and around boulders scattered indiscriminately on the river bed.

It had proved hard to hurry the journey. There had been too much to see, too much to absorb. When he reached the bridge Leo dismounted and sat on the stone coping to consult his map once more. Red moved away to crop hopefully at the belt of brighter green vegetation beside the river. A mile to the west was a low col between two peaks and once there, Madoc mine should be in sight.

In the event, when Leo eventually arrived there, the Madoc slate mine proved to be a disappointment. There was little left to be seen above ground but those roofless stone buildings that the weather had not yet razed.

Leo tethered Red to a thorn bush growing in the open doorway of a derelict hut in which was the remains of an old winding engine, just a pitted drum on a rusting spindle, and set out to explore. Within half an hour it was obvious that he was wasting his time. It had been many a year since Madoc had seen human activity.

The 60-cm rail track which had once linked up the underground workings with the line to Portmadoc, rusted and warped beyond recovery, served as the best indicator to where the old mine entrances, now blocked with slate rubble, had been. There was the remains of an old horse-drawn four-wheeled sledge, once used to ferry the slate blocks up the steep slopes to the surface from the vast underground caverns where the rock-men worked high up on the slate seams, precariously held by a spike and a chain around their thighs so that their hands might be free, setting blasting charges by the naked flame of a candle, working out painfully short, dust-blighted lives. But the good old days had gone and Madoc, like the men who had bought their own tallow candles for the privilege of working it, and the owners who had abandoned it when profit dwindled, was dead.

There was no building that could conceivably have housed the killer in even the remotest degree of comfort, no way that he could have penetrated underground, and no signs of recent occupation. In addition the mine was in clear sight of a minor road that ran from Pentrefoelas to Ffestiniog. It was highly unlikely that anyone seeking a secure hideout would have chosen this spot.

Leo consulted his map and decided to take a slightly different route back. It appeared to be marginally shorter and to select more even terrain. Red was markedly less eager than he had been earlier that morning and it was a mile or two before he accepted the inevitable and put on a good pace.

Some three miles from Madoc Leo caught a glimpse of grey-blue water through a narrow gap between two boulders at the top of a rise he was skirting. He rode up for a better look, intent only on checking his position on the map, and caught sight of a huddle of buildings beside the lake on the floor of the shallow upland valley. Having just left Madoc, he recognized them at once as old mine buildings, and rode out on to the open mountainside for a better look.

The Ordnance Survey map showed the lake and beside it the name 'Garnedd', which presumably was the name of the lake. There was no indication of a mine or of buildings. Certainly this looked a more likely spot for the killer to have chosen. The mine was obviously much smaller than Madoc and was sited well away from the road in an area unlikely to receive many visitors. It was true that there was no sign of life but then, that was hardly to be expected. Garnedd mine was worthy of closer inspection. But not today, he did not want to be absent from Dhys-Gla when the telephone call Colonel Gordon had promised came.

The killer had dug a hole and buried some of his accumulated rubbish, had filled it in and carefully replaced the thin turf, and was returning to his temporary home when he saw the rider up on the far hillside beyond the lake.

For a moment he gave way to panic. No one had ever come to this valley or anywhere near it in the time he had been resident there. Then he forced himself to think clearly. A lone horse rider could offer no serious threat so long as he saw nothing. There was nothing to fear, it was inconceivable that the police would send their men out singly and on horseback.

He ducked behind one of the derelict stone huts and grabbed for the binoculars strung round his neck, a permanent feature of his attire. It was a man, a farmer probably, or more likely a landowner by the look of him, out for a leisurely morning ride. He was working his way across the face of the hill, apparently taking no interest in the mine. No, he was no threat, but a target? Yes, certainly a target, but not here, not right on his own doorstep.

It was with real regret that the killer watched the horseman disappear over the skyline. Such a shot, at the proper range, would have been a real challenge, something different, something to exercise his talents to the full. It would be necessary to gauge the gait of the horse, the rate of travel, the unusual motion of the man's body, and to anticipate the rise and fall of the ground over which he was riding in addition to the usual problems of wind, temperature, air pressure and all the rest. Ah well, it was not to be. Perhaps on some other occasion.

But what a shame, what a pity to lose such a target. There would be few in the world who could make that shot with any hope of success. Make a shot like that and even those stupid thick bastards in the army would know what they were missing. He had been happy and settled in the army, one of an easily identifiable group, part of an *élite*, as he had seen it. Once again though, he had tasted the poison of rejection when, without giving him a fair chance, they had dispensed with his services. Well, now he was showing them just how damned good he was, just how misguided they had been in rejecting him. He was the finest combat shot in the world and by the time he had finished the world would know it.

But his target, although still in sight high up on the slope of the valley and well within his range, was already lost to him. Never mind. He would find another.

The killer remained on watch until he was certain the rider

would not return, then he set about preparing himself for the day's shoot.

'I want to do a deal,' Bennett said.

'I'm listening,' Bob replied.

Once again Bob Staunton was facing Jimmy Bennett across the table in the spartan interview room at Portmadoc Police Station.

'I'll admit the bank jobs, see, but not the murders.'

'Two people died in those bank jobs, didn't they?'

'I don't mean that, I meant the other murders.'

'Okay, Jimmy. Give me his name and you've got a deal.'

'Tony Rees.'

'Where's he from?'

'Swansea, I think.'

'How'd you first meet him, then?'

'I got into trouble in the army. When I got out of Colchester, you know about that . . .'

Bob nodded.

'Well, I went to Birmingham, someone said there was work there, plastering, see. I met Tony in a pub there. We were both broke and he suggested we did a bank.'

'And you agreed.'

'Not just like that. I said no at first but he came here later and found me. He'd got guns, all the gear, like, see. So then I said yes. I didn't think we was going to kill anybody, that's the truth.'

'It just happened.'

'He didn't have no reason to do it really, we was out clear, see?'

'Nutter, is he?' Bob asked.

'Didn't seem to be, not at first. Only when we started I noticed it, when we did the first bank. He seemed to go crazy at the end, even though we'd got the money. I told him about it, like, but he just laughed. He's not so tough you know, not really, I think he's scared, but when he's got a gun, if we're on a job, seems he's just got to use that gun, see?'

'Has he got a rifle?' Bob asked.

158

'Yes. I saw him with it.'

'Good shot, is he?'

'Pretty good. Saw him shooting at pine cones, see. Didn't miss that I saw.'

'Okay Jimmy, what's his address?'

'No address. He's living rough. Says it's safer that way. Only luck I know where he is . . .'

'How's that?'

'He never wanted me to know where he was, see. We only met when he'd set a job up. I got worried about that, didn't seem right he could find me and I couldn't find him, so after the last job I followed him, that's when I saw him firing the rifle.'

'So where is he?'

'You get a map and I'll show you . . .'

When Leo arrived back at Dhys-Gla at 10 a.m. a slight drizzle had started. As he dismounted in the farmyard Nerys came running out to greet him, ignoring the rain, throwing her arms around his neck and holding him tightly to her, covering him with kisses then burying her face in his neck.

'I must go out more often,' Leo laughed.

'You must not. I've been worried to death.'

'No need. I didn't see a living soul.'

'I'm glad.'

'I'm not. I had some hopes I might come across something at the mine.'

She kept tight hold of him as he led the tired horse across the farmyard to the stable block.

'I took a slightly different route on the way back,' Leo said. 'A mile or so to the south I came across a small valley about three miles from Madoc. There was a lake and some mine workings, old derelict buildings like those at Madoc but this mine was obviously much smaller.'

'That would be Garnedd.'

'Yes, I saw that name on the map. I wondered why you did not mention it.'

'It's so small, not a proper mine. There are hundreds of small workings like Garnedd which never made money and were abandoned as soon as they discovered the slate was poor quality or the seam was not thick enough or the transport problem was too great to make it pay.'

'It looked interesting to me, more interesting than Madoc because it is so well hidden. I think I might take a look at it tomorrow.'

'Do you have to, Leo?' Nerys asked as they walked across the farmyard to the house.

'We have to find this man, Nerys, before he kills someone else.'

'I know. But don't expect me to like the idea.'

Having settled Red into the stable they repaired to the farm kitchen where Morwenna made a cup of tea for them and it was only with the greatest difficulty that Leo was able to dissuade her from cooking him another breakfast. When the telephone rang, Leo won the race to answer it.

'I am expecting a call,' he explained.

'Mr Leo Wyndsor, please.' It was a man's voice, cultured and confident.

'Speaking.'

'Ah, excellent. I understand you visited a friend of mine in Exeter recently, John Gordon?'

'Yes, I did.'

'Then no doubt you will have been expecting me to contact you.'

'Yes, indeed,' Leo said. 'John told you what I was interested to know?'

'He did. The only chap I can think of who fits the bill left us just over a year ago.'

The line twanged and whined, suggesting the call was long distance. 'His name?' Leo enquired, taking out a ballpoint pen with one hand and pulling the telephone notepad towards him.

'Yes, David Albert Pike.'

'Can you tell me his last known address?'

'Married man, home address, 107 Wanstead Vale, Birmingham.'

'Age?'

'He'd be thirty-two now.'

'And he was trained by John Gordon?'

'No, but at the same school, before John's time. I had him in my unit for nine months.'

'Can you tell me why he left you, I gather he had no option about that?'

'No, he had no option, he was required to leave. He was guilty of something the official jargon calls "indiscriminate targetting", you understand?'

'He liked killing people.'

There was a moment's silence. 'Rather bluntly put but accurate, I should say. We formed the opinion that he was psychologically unsuited to the work.'

'Do you happen to know if he has any contacts in, or knowledge of, North Wales?'

'Well, his place of birth is shown as Llangollen but he was married when he first joined us, served for six years in all, and the only address we ever had was the one I have given you. I understand it is the home of his wife's parents and the records show he declined married quarters.'

'So they were living apart?'

'So it seems, but we have no record of a divorce. Anything else I can help you with?'

'Not at the moment. If anything else comes up I will contact John Gordon and perhaps he will be kind enough to put us in touch again.'

'I'm sure he would do that.'

'I'm very grateful for your help,' Leo said.

He replaced the receiver only to pick it up again immediately and dial the number of the incident room at Portmadoc. He asked for Chief Superintendent Davies but it was Sergeant Richards who eventually answered.

'Mr Davies and Mr Staunton are out, sir,' he told Leo. 'Bennett talked and they've taken a team out to bring his mate in.' Richards sounded considerably put out that he had not been included in the posse.

'Did Bennett give them a name?' Leo asked.

'Yes, sir. They man they're after is called Tony Rees.'

'Are we certain of the name?'

'That's the name Bennett gave, sir.'

Leo thought rapidly. 'Look, Gwyn,' he said, 'you remember that army enquiry?'

'Yes?'

'I have just spoken to them again. It is possible that Tony Rees is in fact an ex-sniper named David Pike. Pike was discharged for being psychologically unfit just over a year ago. He was born at Llangollen and trained at Exeter where the rifle and ammunition were stolen. The only address we have is in Birmingham, can you take it down . . .'

'Yes, sir. Fire away.'

Leo rattled off the address, then said: 'Ask Birmingham police to contact his wife and find out as much about Pike as they can, then get them to put her on the first train to Portmadoc. If Rees is in fact Pike she will be able to tell us. If she can give us his parents' address in Llangollen, check that as well. Ask Birmingham to treat this as urgent and ring me back here as soon as you can, will you?'

'Yes, sir.'

As he replaced the receiver Nerys appeared from the kitchen.

'Is everything all right, dear?' she asked.

'Yes, everything is fine,' Leo said.

Of the twenty officers who went to arrest Tony Rees, only Bob Staunton was unarmed. He assured Chief Superintendent Davies that with a gun in his hand he was of far more danger to himself than the enemy.

The raid had been planned with some care. Rees had holed up well away from any roads and the hut he had built himself was hidden in a dense clump of trees in a shallow valley. It was an easily defensible spot and if no officers were to die, surprise was essential. Accordingly, the Landrovers that transported them stopped a good mile short of their destination.

By 11.30 a.m. Rees' hideout was ringed with police, closing in on foot, halting, as instructed, along the rim of the valley. The weather favoured them. It was dull and overcast with the occasional spot of rain. Bob Staunton was hardly in his element. The mile hike had seemed like ten to him and by the time he took up his position beside Ewen Davies at the lowest point of the valley rim, he was blowing hard and in no good humour.

When the valley had been surrounded without incident, Davies called together six armed men, wearing issue bulletproof jackets, and sent them to take up positions further down the slope towards the tree clump. He and Bob crouched behind a rock, watching the officers progress down the valley side, waiting for them to get into position before they called Rees out.

'Hate sending kids into a thing like this,' Davies said.

'Wouldn't do no good us going, would it?' Bob commented. 'Fat lot of good we'd be down there.'

The six officers took what cover they could but had no training in fieldcraft and if Rees was at all alert he would have had no real trouble in spotting them. In fact they were within twenty yards of the trees, spaced out around the perimeter, when the whip-crack of the rifle shot reverberated round the valley, shattering the quiet and bringing fierce oaths from Staunton and Davies. Below them an officer rolled on the ground clutching his leg.

Davies brought the megaphone he had been holding up to his mouth. 'Rees ... this is the police ...' His voice bellowed out round the shallow valley. 'We are armed and you are completely surrounded. Come out with your arms above your head ...'

Davies lowered the megaphone and waited. But there was no sound from the valley floor. Davies tried again, repeating his words slowly and carefully.

The sudden, unexpected staccato scream of the motor-cycle engine stunned the watching officers into immobility. The trials bike erupted out of the clump of trees and, picking up speed on the flat, headed straight for the lowest edge of the valley rim, where Bob Staunton and Ewen Davies stood.

'Bloody hell!' Davies swore.

He put the megaphone to his mouth again. 'All officers, leave cover,' he commanded.

All round the rim of the valley armed officers stood up in the open. But they were impotent. They could not shoot a man who was simply trying to escape, no matter what crimes he had committed before that moment.

Certainly, if Rees saw them, he took not the slightest notice. The trials bike was scudding up the slope towards Davies and Staunton and now they could see the rifle slung across the rider's back.

Davies scrambled down the slope at an angle, intent on cutting Rees off, with Bob Staunton making slower progress behind him. Now Rees was heading straight towards them, hunched over the handlebars, clearly with no intention of stopping.

Ewen Davies put the megaphone to his mouth again. 'Give up, Rees,' he shouted. 'Give up or we fire.'

If Rees could hear above the high-pitched whine of the trials engine he gave no sign, simply held the throttle wide open as the bike bounded up the slope towards Davies' portly figure.

Davies, seeing that commands and entreaties would have no effect and that if he remained where he was Rees would run him down, hurled the megaphone at the speeding figure and dived for cover. Rees swerved his machine to avoid the missile, but it barely slowed his progress.

Bob Staunton felt anger and frustration boiling up in him. The nearest police vehicle was more than a mile away and if Rees got clear of the valley his escape was certain. It would take a nation-wide manhunt to find him again. More from anger than hope Bob picked a loose rock and hurled it down the slope into the path of the fleeing motor-cycle.

The rock bounced once, then struck the front wheel of the speeding machine, smashing spokes and knocking the wheel sideways. As the machine cartwheeled, Rees was thrown forward over the handlebars and hurled to the ground.

He was still conscious but momentarily stunned. His recovery was rapid. As he began to scramble to his feet he slipped the rifle off his shoulder, ready to bring it into play.

Then Davies was standing over him, a revolver held steady in his hand.

'You just try it, boy,' he said, 'and I'll blow your bloody head off, see?'

Sergeant Richards telephoned Leo Wyndsor at Dhys-Gla at midday. Leo had been fidgeting about the house, waiting for the call, aware of a mounting excitement tinged with apprehension, aware that the hunt was coming to a climax, irritated that circumstances had left him so far from the action. When he answered the telephone, however, his voice was deliberately calm.

'Yes, Gwyn?'

'Birmingham police have interviewed Mrs Pike, sir. She will arrive at Bangor tonight. I'll arrange to have her picked up and brought here.'

'What did she say?'

'She's not seen her husband for two years. She's trying to get a divorce but she's not been able to find him, so she's quite happy to come here and identify him. Apparently his parents died about seven years ago, that's confirmed by the Llangollen police. She gave us the address. The present owners of the house have never heard of David Pike or Tony Rees.'

'Was Pike violent at home, was that the reason for the separation?'

'No. Quite the reverse, sir. She said he was as quiet as a mouse, never raised his voice to her.'

'What went wrong with the marriage, then?'

'Seems he just lost interest. Mrs Pike said he was a nut about guns and shooting. Thought more about his guns than he did about her, she says. Anyway, she's got herself a boy-friend now, wants rid of Pike, see.'

'That will suit us very well, thank you, Gwyn. Are Mr Davies and Mr Staunton back yet?'

'No, sir. But we have had a message to say that they have Rees, or Pike, if that's who he is, in custody. One of our P.C.s got shot in the leg but that's all we've heard.'

'Right, Gwyn. When they get back tell them what we have found out. I shall be at Portmadoc myself in about half an hour.'

'Very well, sir.'

Leo replaced the receiver and went out to the paddock where he knew he would find Nerys. She was running Merry round on a long rein, encouraging the mare to run off some of the fat she had accumulated from inactivity. Nerys saw Leo coming and walked across to meet him at the gate.

'I have to go into Portmadoc, darling,' Leo said.

'Something has happened?' Nerys asked anxiously.

'We have a man in custody in connection with the murders.'

'Leo . . . that's marvellous!'

'Yes, it is.'

'Can I take Merry out, then? She's getting so fat and lazy . . .'

'Not quite yet.'

'Why? Leo . . . it's not just Merry, I seem to have been cooped up here for ages. Morwenna and I didn't even go to church this morning because you were . . . I mean, we thought it better not to go. Surely if you have arrested this man . . .'

'I want to make certain, darling. Surely you can restrain yourself for another hour or so. I will telephone you as soon as I know exactly what the position is.'

'Oh, very well. You will telephone me?'

'I said so. Now, I must go.'

'I'll come and see you off.'

They walked back to the farmhouse, arms round each other's waists.

'When will you be back?' Nerys asked.

'I'm not sure. Certainly for dinner tonight, I hope.'

'And then it will all be over?'

'It seems likely.'

'Then you'll go back to London, will you?'

'Only for as long as it takes to arrange some leave. Daffyd said I could come back for a holiday whenever I liked. I shall have to come back for the trial anyway. Have you said anything to your father, about us?'

'No. But he knows. I suspect he knew the first day you arrived.'

'Which is more than I did! I have a bottle of whisky in my

case, I keep it for emergencies. I think I will bring it down after dinner tonight and we can tell the family.'

'Oh, so getting married to me is an emergency, is it?' Nerys said, laughing.

Leo kissed her. 'Don't be difficult,' he ordered. 'We tell the family tonight.'

'Yes,' Nerys agreed happily, 'we'll tell them tonight.'

Leo found Bob Staunton and Ewen Davies in great good spirits when he arrived at the Portmadoc incident room. They were in Davies' office, poring over a collection of weapons found in the hut Rees had occupied.

'Congratulations, sir,' Leo said with a touch of envy. 'It looks as if you have struck gold.'

'So we did, mate,' Bob said, 'so we did.'

'Has Gwyn Richards told you about David Pike and the information from Birmingham?'

'He did,' Davies answered. 'It looks very much as if Rees is in fact Pike. That was an inspired guess you had about contacting the army.'

'Ties all the loose ends up nicely, don't it?' Bob confirmed. 'You was worried that Rees didn't have the trainin' to do these murders, weren't you?'

'I was, yes. Did you find the rifle?'

'Yeah,' Bob confirmed. 'Had it on him when he tried to make a break. It's gone off to the lab to be test fired.'

'Does it have a scopesight?' Leo asked.

'No, mate. But don't worry about that. Rees's got a cache somewhere 'cos we ain't found his share of the loot from the bank jobs yet.'

'The rifle is a .62 mm, is it?' Leo enquired.

'It's a rifle, we ain't experts ... but I'll tell you somethin', there's marks on the barrel where it's had a scopesight fitted sometime and Jimmy Bennett reckons he's seen Rees knock pine cones out of a tree easy as kiss my bum. That cheer you up, does it?'

'Has he admitted the murders?' Leo asked.

'He will. At the moment he's doin' a Greta Garbo act but he ain't had time to get over the shock of gettin' nicked yet.'

'Well, that seems to be that . . .'

'You actually agree we got the right bloke then, do you?' Bob asked, grinning.

'Well . . . provided that Mrs Pike identifies the man we have as her husband . . .'

Bob looked at Davies and adopted a pained expression. 'See what I have to put up with, Ewen,' he said. 'Black and white aren't good enough, he wants it in full colour.'

Davies grinned.

Leo made a gesture of defeat. 'I give in,' he said. 'I'll just go and see Gwyn Richards, find out exactly what time Mrs Pike is due to arrive.'

In the main incident office Leo obtained the information from Sergeant Richards, then telephoned Dhys-Gla. Nerys must have been standing by the phone waiting for the call.

'Leo . . .?' she enquired.

'You were expecting some other man to ring?' Leo enquired in mock suspicion.

'Don't be silly . . . is everything all right?'

'Yes. It looks as if we have our man. There are just a few ends to tie up.'

'Then you will be back tonight, for dinner?'

'As I promised. I must go now . . . until tonight.'

'I miss you,' Nerys said.

Leo was collecting one or two knowing grins from the officers in the incident room. Slightly embarrassed he said: 'I feel exactly the same way.'

When he returned to Davies' office the exhibits officer was labelling and packing up the weapons on the desk and Bob and Ewen Davies were putting on their coats.

'Time to feed the inner man,' Bob announced. 'You comin', Leo?'

Leo shrugged. 'Well, there is nothing I can do here, it seems . . .'

'You don't seem very keen, boy,' Davies put in. 'Got other plans, have you?'

'He's got this bit of crumpet at the farm,' Bob confided. 'I ain't seen her yet but she's got him sweatin' all right. He's been bloody useless ever since we got here.'

'Oh, yes?' Davies said. 'Serious, is it?'

'It is,' Leo admitted.

'Let him go off and see her then, Bob,' Davies suggested. 'There's nothing we need him for at the moment, is there?'

'Too right, mate. He's in a dream anyway. Go on Leo, push off, son. I'll give you a ring later.'

'Well, if you are sure, sir . . .'

'Tell this bird of yours I'll be over there to eat tomorrow night. I want to give her the once-over, know what I mean? Tell her to do the cookin' . . . don't want you married to no toffee-nosed bit what can't feed a man proper, do we?'

Leo smiled uncertainly, wondering what the family would make of Bob Staunton. 'I will arrange it,' he promised.

Bob hesitated by the door. 'They don't dress up for dinner or nothin' like that, do they?' he asked.

'No. We eat in the kitchen.'

Bob visibly brightened. 'Ah, well,' he said, 'sounds all right then, don't it?'

Pike had left his camp at Garnedd mine at dawn that morning heading almost due north, towards Pont-y-plant. He had no roads to cross and despite the persistent drizzle he made good time.

He had deliberately chosen this direction because it took him well away from the locations of the previous shootings, helping to spread his activities and blur any pattern. His only concern was that the weather should clear; he did not favour exposing his cherished rifle to the rain and in any event, shooting in such poor conditions became something of a lottery, and was no fair test of man or equipment.

In the thick forest bordering the peak of Ro-Wen he stopped

to rest and when he recommenced his journey the rain had stopped, although the day was still overcast. From here on he could afford to take a target of opportunity, but for a long while he saw no one, the weather had deterred all but the stout-hearted.

By half past ten he had taken up position on a peak that lay almost equidistant between Dolwyddelan to the west and Pen-machno to the east, where he had a good all-round view. But still no target presented itself. He did not care to travel further, or to move any closer to either town, so he summoned up his store of patience and settled down to wait.

It was a little before midday when he first saw the group of walkers. There were five of them, dressed alike in heavy walking boots and waterproof anoraks and they were perhaps two miles away, heading towards him. Not only did they represent the only target he was likely to meet that day but they afforded an interesting study in careful target selection and precision shoot-ing. Part of his training had been to select and hit brief targets in congested urban areas where an error meant the death of a civi-lian and the escape of an enemy. True, this was a rural and not an urban area and the walkers were separated by several feet, but the conditions were bad, rendering the shot more difficult.

He would close in and shoot from 400 yards. That was fair range under the conditions, fair for him, fair for the target. He opened the carrying case and began to assemble the rifle, keeping one eye on the advancing walkers.

When the rifle was assembled to his satisfaction, Pike moved off down the slope, rifle in one hand and carrying case in the other, looking out for a suitable firing spot. He left the carrying case behind a prominent rock on the line of his retreat, then moved forward more quickly, taking greater care to secure cover now that he was within a mile of his quarry.

He settled into a slight hollow three-quarters of the way down the mountainside and busied himself with preparations for the shot. Light conditions were bad but there was virtually no wind. The leader of the approaching group was not more than half a mile away now, there was no time for finesse. This first walker was wearing a yellow anorak, the others brown and green. Pike discarded the leader as too easy a shot. He made minute adjustments to the telescopic sight as he selected his target and finally settled on the third figure in line.

The ground was damp and uncomfortable. Now that he was in position the walkers seemed to have slowed down, but that surely was just his imagination. Pike took a single bullet from his jacket pocket, gave it a final polish with a scrap of cloth, then loaded it.

He ran the eye of the scopesight down the line of walkers, picked out his selected target and locked on. He exhaled slowly until his whole body was motionless, not a muscle flickering, then he gently took up the four-pound pressure on the trigger.

His target was flung backwards and sideways as the bullet struck and then lay still on the ground. The other walkers stood in frozen tableau for a second, then clustered around their fallen comrade. Pike watched dispassionately. They were staring about them now, pointing and gesticulating, he could just catch the shock and terror in their voices. Then they picked up the dead man and, bunched together, hastened away towards the nearest tree line.

Pike waited until they had disappeared into the forest, then returned to the rock where he had left the carrying case and packed the rifle away. He was vaguely dissatisfied with the shot. It had, after all, proved rather too easy.

Leo arrived at Dhys-Gla at two o'clock. As he came in the front door he met Daffyd in the hall, dressed in his Sunday suit and looking unusually smart.

'Leo . . . didn't expect you back so soon, boy.'

'Just a flying visit,' Leo said. 'I found myself with an hour to spare.'

'Well, we had lunch early, see, not expecting you. But you'll have something with us now, Morwenna will find you something.'

Suddenly it seemed a very long time since his pre-dawn breakfast. 'Yes, thank you, Daffyd. I'll just ring the office first though, if I may, just to make sure everything is in order there,' Leo said.

'Certainly my boy, certainly.'

The telephone in the incident room rang for some time before Sergeant Richards answered it.

'There's a big flap on, sir,' he told Leo. 'Mr Davies and Mr Staunton are getting a team together. There's been another killing out in the Gwydyr Forest.'

'Is that certain?' said Leo incredulously.

'Yes. The same as the others. I was just about to ring you. Mr Staunton said for you to meet him there.'

'You have the exact location?'

'Yes, map reference . . .'

'Wait, hang on Gwyn, let me make a note of it.'

Leo scribbled the information down on the telephone pad, then pulled his map from his pocket. 'How long ago?' he asked.

'About twelve o'clock, as far as we can gather, perhaps just after.'

'Gwyn, give me a moment to think,' Leo said.

The news had come as a shock. Like everyone else engaged on the enquiry Leo had accepted that the killer was already in custody. Now it was abundantly clear that the killer was Pike and that he had no connection whatsoever with Rees or Bennett. Leo swore under his breath as he inspected his map. What had he been thinking of? Now someone else had died and it had been preventable. He had been doubtful of the involvement of the bank robbers in the type of murder they were investigating. He should have stuck to his guns. Going to the scene of the murder would not help, Pike was on his way back to his base. And Leo was certain now that he knew where that base was. Pike would not risk his precious rifle in a ramshackle hut. He was dry and safe. He was underground.

'Gwyn . . .'

'Yes, sir?'

'Do you know the old Madoc mine, a few miles outside Ffestiniog?'

'Yes, vaguely.'

'Wait, I'll give you the map reference . . .' Leo rattled off the figures. 'Get hold of Mr Davies and Mr Staunton, tell them I said to drum up a team of armed men, as many as they can raise, and meet me there ... better bring Landrovers, it's rough country.'

'You think he's at the Madoc mine, sir?'

'No. I think we shall find him, or at least his base, a couple of miles further west, a smaller mine beside Lake Garnedd ...' he read off the map reference. 'Tell them to hurry, I shall leave immediately and meet them there.'

Leo slammed down the phone and ran into the kitchen. Daffyd, Morwenna and young Jones looked at him in astonishment.

'What is it, Leo?' Daffyd asked.

'Something urgent has come up, Daffyd. I have to rush off. Say goodbye to Nerys for me.'

'She's gone out, Leo ...'

'Out? She promised me she would stay in the house.'

'But she's been confined to the farm for days ... Merry needed exercise, you said you'd caught the man so we saw no harm in her going out for a ride, see.'

The fear that had been lurking in Leo's stomach now flooded his body, leaving him weak.

'Where has she gone?' he asked.

'She said she was taking the same route you took the other day, towards the old Madoc mine ... Leo, you're as white as a sheet, what is it, boy?'

Leo laid the map on the kitchen table and stared at it. 'How long has she been gone?' he asked thickly.

'Not long.' Daffyd glanced at the clock on the mantelpiece above the kitchen range. 'Not yet an hour.'

Leo's hand shook as he picked up the map. 'The killer is still loose, Daffyd ...' His voice was fractured with despair.

'Leo?'

'He shot someone near Gwydyr Forest just after twelve o'clock today. If he is heading straight back to his base, if he is living where I think he is, then Nerys will ride right across his path ...'

173

CHAPTER TWELVE

Leo tore his car out of the farmyard and screamed down the narrow tree-shrouded track towards the road, driving like a madman. He could not follow Nerys on horseback, it would be far too slow, nor could he hope to follow her by the route she had taken if he used his car. His best, his only hope was to drive to Madoc mine, meet up with the other officers in the Landrovers there, then drive straight to the killer's hideout at Garnedd.

If Pike was not there, then he could drive back along the route Nerys was taking, hoping to meet her. If, when he arrived at Garnedd, search revealed that Pike did not have his base there, then Leo had nothing to fear, only a good deal of explaining to do. But Leo knew with a dread certainty that this would not be the case. His every instinct told him that Nerys was in grave danger and that soon he and Pike would meet face to face. He had one stop to make though, on his way to Madoc mine. Bare hands would not protect Nerys against a target rifle and if he arrived at Madoc before the others he had no intention of waiting.

Leo ground the car to a halt outside Major Thomas' cottage, hit the horn, then ran to the front door and hammered on it. Owen Thomas stared at the distraught figure but was given no time to ask questions.

Leo showed his warrant card. 'Owen, Daffyd told you who I am?'

'Yes.'

'I want your target rifle and ammunition, and a torch. I want them this instant. Nerys is in danger.'

Owen Thomas still stared at him.

'For God's sake, man! Move yourself!' Leo shouted.

Thomas came out of his stupor. 'Wait here,' he said, 'I won't be a second.'

He ran down the hall and out into the back garden to the old underground shelter that housed his weapons. It seemed to Leo that he was gone an age. When he returned he had a long black-handled torch, the target rifle fitted with a scopesight and a box of ammunition.

'You do know how to use this?' he asked, as he handed over the rifle.

But Leo grabbed the equipment from him and rushed back to his car without a word. Then there was a spurt of wet gravel and the car shot back on to the road.

It was as well that Leo met no traffic on the minor roads that led him to Madoc mine. He simply pressed the accelerator to the floorboards and left it there, using all the road on the corners. The modest and rather staid saloon was not used to such treatment. It bucked and weaved, leaning hard over on its springs on the bends, shivering and shaking with effort on the straight.

As soon as he saw the Madoc mine workings Leo turned off the road and headed the car out across the open upland grass. He did not stop at the mine because it was evident that Staunton and Davies had not yet arrived. He would have no choice but to get as far as he could in his own car, unsuitable as it was for this terrain.

His progress was now unavoidably slower and as the ground began to rise the wheels spun and slipped and the engine whined in protest. He drove round the side of the hills that surrounded Garnedd valley, looking for an entrance, gaining height all the time by a crablike forward and upward movement. He had all but given up hope and prepared to continue on foot when he saw a break in the rock rim and headed towards it.

As the slope steepened and the wheels spun, the car gradually lost momentum. The speedometer was registering zero when, with a final desperate play on clutch and accelerator, Leo forced the vehicle up on to the ridge and hesitated, looking down into the valley.

There was no wind, not a ripple on the surface of the lake. The water was iron grey beneath the clouds which still threatened rain and the thin reeds at the water's edge stood still and upright. There was no movement amongst the scattering of derelict stone buildings huddled between the lake and the single mine entrance in the hillside except for a fluttering of birds amongst the grass.

The valley was shallow and the route down to lake level easy but for the tufts of black rock sprouting from the thin green mantle on the slopes. Leo held the car in second gear and picked a fast downward path through the outcroppings of rock, aiming to arrive on the valley floor near the mine working for fear of soft ground near the lake edge.

There was no time for caution. He stopped the car suddenly amongst the slate tips and roofless outbuildings, rapidly loaded the rifle, then stood out in the open and shouted a challenge.

'Pike ... you're finished ... come out ... Pike ...'

His only answer was the angry twittering of a cloud of small birds that rose from the reeds behind him. He ran forward to the mine entrance. It was barred by a rough door of galvanized sheeting on a heavy wooden frame and the huge rusted padlock had clearly not been touched for years. But the grass around the entrance was a slightly different colour from the rest, bruised by a regular tread.

Leo stood back, worked the bolt action, put the rifle to his shoulder and fired into the doorway. The bullet left a neat hole in the metal sheeting and the shot echoed round the valley but elicited no response. Leo moved forward to inspect the door. On one side the screws holding the rusted hinges had been removed,

176

the double door could be moved out of position in one section. There was no point in retreating now.

Leo hauled the door away from the entrance and entered the gaping blackness of the mine shaft. The floor was uneven and the roof sloped downwards to one side. Leo switched on his torch and moved forward, holding it away from his body to make himself less of a target. Thirty yards from the tunnel entrance the powerful torch was straining to penetrate the solid blackness that surrounded him. It was cold and somewhere water was dripping into water with a monotonous rhythm.

Coming to the entrance to a side tunnel, Leo halted, but the torch revealed that it was blocked by a fall of rock. Now there was water running by his feet, an inch or so deep, occupying a shallow dip at the side of the shaft. The shaft sloped downwards and the deeper he went the more fear prickled Leo's neck and greased his palms with sweat. If Pike was waiting for him down here he stood little chance of survival. Only a greater fear for Nerys' safety drove him on.

Then his torch picked out a low tunnel on his right. A baulk of timber had been wedged in position above it and a thick curtain of waterproof sheeting hung down, closing off the opening. Leo moved forward and covered the entrance with his rifle.

'You are finished, Pike,' he called. 'Come out, the valley is surrounded by armed police.'

The lie echoed back down the shaft, mocking him, provoking only silence. Leo now had no options but retreat or frontal attack. Before fear could slow him he thrust the sheeting aside and dived into the opening, holding the torch and rifle ahead of him.

The low-roofed cave, once an exploratory tunnel, was no more than ten feet long, five feet wide and six feet high. At the far end, in a corner, was a roughly made wooden frame bed with blankets and a sleeping bag. There was a rucksack, boxes of food, a portable stove, cans of gas fuel, some clothing, a plastic bucket containing water, but no occupant.

Leo conducted a rapid search. He found three rounds of highly polished 7.62 mm ammunition but no rifle, no carrying case, no scopesight. Pike had not yet returned from his latest killing, or if he had, he had gone looking for another target. Leo blundered back out into the main shaft and set off at a scrambling run towards the tunnel entrance.

Even the dull light of the clouded day blinded him momentarily as he emerged from the depths of the hillside. He ran to the car and abandoned all caution as he threw the protesting vehicle round the lower slopes of the valley, heading for the gap in the rock rim. He was totally distraught now, sick with fear, driving on instinct.

His only hope was to find Nerys before Pike did. He had no doubt that if he failed, Nerys was as good as dead. He was crying with anger and frustration, banging senselessly at the steering wheel in a futile attempt to force more speed from the car, screaming his frustration aloud into the silence of the valley.

Pike had not hurried his return journey. He had been thinking. Some sixth sense warned him that he should abandon his operation soon, even if he had not used up all the ammunition he had. There had been no sign of the net closing on him but for some reason, perhaps the detention by the police of the unknown man about whom the radio had said no more, he now felt hunted in a way he had not previously.

He had learnt over the years to obey his instinct. It was time to retreat, let things cool off, see a few Westerns, hibernate amongst humanity for the winter months. Come the spring he could plan a new campaign.

He was some three miles from Garnedd mine when he first saw the horse and rider. The binoculars told him it was a woman. She seemed in no hurry, following the lower ground, heading in the same direction as he had been, perhaps a mile to his right. They were on convergent courses and would pass in twenty minutes or so.

Pike hesitated. He had promised himself such a shot. But they would be close to Garnedd, too close. Would that matter now, though? If he intended to leave anyway, now was as good a time as any. He could be packed and gone before the body was found, it might not be found for days in this wasteland of hills. The temptation to take a last target was strong, in the end too strong for him to resist. He turned his mind seriously to the problem, examining the ground ahead, looking for a suitable firing position.

If he moved fast and kept to the high ground he could take a position ahead of her and to her left well before she was within suitable range. The clouds were heavier now, rain was imminent, the light was bad. He thought a range of 200 yards would be right, given all the circumstances. But he must hurry. Precision with speed was what this shot required.

Pike picked up the camouflaged carrying case and set off at a loping run, stopping only now and then to ensure that the target had not changed direction or turned back.

Nerys was happy. Leo had caught his murderer and was safe. She let Merry find her own way and allowed her thoughts to wander, lost in a lotus dream.

How short a time she had known Leo. How little she knew of him. How did he vote? Did he snore? Was he tolerant, loyal, strong, as she hoped, as she thought he must be? That night, at Dhys-Gla, they would tell the family that they were to marry. Two strangers, binding themselves together for a lifetime. She shrugged off that thought. Time was irrelevant. She knew Leo, knew him totally. She loved him.

What of his parents? He had never spoken of them. Were they still alive? How dreadful if they did not like her or think her good enough for their son. But that was silly. She was creating difficulties where, in all probability, none existed. She should be thinking of more practical matters, such as finding someone to deal with the paperwork on the smallholding when she was no longer there. Father would never cope.

That was what she should be doing. But it was far more pleasant to think of Leo, and to dream, leaving Merry to make the decisions.

Leo managed to curse and kick the car for just over a mile before it finally bogged down in a marshy area below a ridge. When he realized that the cause was hopeless, he feverishly grabbed the rifle and set off on a desperate scrambling run up the facing slope. What had seemed an easy rise from a distance proved to be a hard, lung-searing climb that soon left him exhausted and gasping for breath.

He drove himself past the pain barrier with an effort of sheer will, forcing his anguished muscles to work on when they were screaming for rest. When he reached the top of the ridge his hands were torn and bleeding, his clothing ripped and dirtied, and his face ashen and pain-scarred.

Unbelievably, there she was. It had to be her, who else would be riding up here? She was still a mile away, heading towards him, just one more low ridge separating them. Relief flooded through Leo's body, weakening him so that he stumbled and almost fell.

He waved the rifle and tried to shout but could raise no power from his thudding lungs. She had not seen him. But she was safe.

Leo began to run, lurching drunkenly down the slope of the ridge until, at the bottom, Nerys was for the moment hidden from his sight.

Pike lay prone on the ground, the canvas strap of the target rifle wrapped tightly round his left arm, the slim, camouflaged barrel burdened with the scopesight pointing out from behind a rock. He made a final finicky adjustment to the scopesight before settling its rubber cup around his right eye. He was totally absorbed in the shot, his concentration absolute.

There was no wind to bother him, only the poor light caused him concern. The girl was coming on at a steady pace, looking neither right nor left. She seemed to be indifferent to her surroundings, as if she were in a dream.

He centred the fine crossed wires of the scopesight on her chest, relaxed, expelled his breath and squeezed gently on the trigger.

CHAPTER THIRTEEN

Leo mounted the last ridge separating him from Nerys and stood at the top, chest heaving, eyes fixed on her approaching figure. She was no more than 300 yards away, surely she must see him standing against the skyline? But she gave no sign of recognition.

Then a slight movement up on the hillside to his right attracted his attention. It could have been a rabbit, or a bird alighting but it set alarm bells ringing in Leo's head. He stared at the spot fiercely until finally he recognized the outline of a man's head against a sunken rock some 200 yards away, the face partly obscured by the stock and telescopic sight of a powerful rifle. The man was aiming at the oncoming girl.

For what seemed an eternity Leo was incapable of movement, stunned by the impending horror. Then he was screaming at the man and bringing his rifle up to his shoulder in ungainly haste.

The whipcrack of the two shots followed one close upon the other. Then the girl and the horse were down and even at that distance Leo could see a bright splash of blood across the upper part of Nerys' body. Bursting rage overtook him. He was a wild animal, as insane as the man he had been hunting. Holding the rifle forward in both hands, as if he intended a bayonet charge, Leo began a crazed, lumbering run up the hillside towards the killer.

'Pike!' he yelled. 'Pike, I'm going to kill you . . .'

The shot fired by Leo Wyndsor had missed its target by a long way but had fractionally distracted Pike as he was in the very act of firing. Nonetheless, the shot was good, the target was down. The girl had hit the grass and stayed there. Pike had a glimpse of a blood splash across her face. He took the merest fraction of time to make that assessment as he rolled sideways to cover himself from the unexpected attack, working the bolt action of the rifle as he did so.

His movements were automatic, putting solid rock between himself and a bullet was second nature. But he was for a moment confused and frightened. Something had gone badly wrong and his first sight of his attacker did nothing to help his understanding of events.

The big blond-haired man seemed to have gone berserk. He was scrambling up the slope towards Pike shouting his name . . . how the hell did he know the name? In the man's right hand was a very useful-looking target rifle. He recognized him now. He was the one who had ridden into the valley that morning. The blond hair was unmistakable. Who was he? What was he to the girl? Could he be a policeman? Surely not; the police did not carry target rifles.

Pike looked quickly about him. There was no time for hesitation. The man was alone. He had to die. Pike stood, settled the butt of the rifle into his shoulder, sighted on the scrambling, incoherent figure below him. It was an easy shot. He did not, for once, take particular care.

He saw his target fall and lie still. He watched for a second but there was no movement. He looked quickly to his right but the horse and the girl had not moved. He returned his attention to the fallen man whose outstretched hand was a foot away from the rifle he had put to such poor use. Pike began to go down the slope. The shot had been hasty. He could not afford to leave the man or the girl alive. A bullet through the head would be the best insurance he could have. He stopped six feet from the man's body and raised the rifle to his shoulder.

He felt the thud of the bullet when it struck his side but he was prostrate on the ground before he heard the whipcrack of the shot. He felt no pain. His mind was a blank. He could not understand what had happened.

It was as much exhaustion and shock as the bullet that hit him in the upper thigh that had felled Leo Wyndsor. That and a crushing knowledge of utter failure. He lay unmoving, his eyes open and staring, his mind stunned.

The second shot woke him from his stupor. He rolled over and eased himself into a sitting position, seeing Pike stretched out on the ground near him and on the ridge 100 yards away two figures standing beside a police Landrover – one of them unmistakably Bob Staunton, the other, uniformed, still with the rifle raised.

Leo struggled to his feet. There was a dull pain in his left thigh and a blinding ache at the back of his neck. He could see that Pike was moving his hands towards his precious rifle lying just out of reach. He picked up his own rifle and worked the bolt action. He watched Pike dispassionately, his rage spent. He felt only pain and emptiness.

Pike was nothing special to look at. Average was the only word to describe him. Even in his camouflaged clothing, with his face blackened and streaked for war, he seemed no more dangerous than a second-rate actor dressed for the part. His fingers were a bare inch from the rifle now, his face distorted with effort. Maimed as he was, his every instinct drove him to recover the weapon. Pike was a killer to the last.

Leo Wyndsor waited. He could have disarmed the man, although he himself was injured, but he made no attempt to do so. His mind was utterly clear in those seconds, he knew exactly what the law permitted. Although his weapons training had, in the event, proved quite inadequate for the situation in which he found himself, Leo had Sergeant Callis to thank for the model exposition of justifiable homicide. He could only kill Pike if Pike was in the act of endangering life. In the act. So breathlessly Leo waited for Pike to encompass his own death, waited with cold, bitter determination, his face rigid with hate.

Pike had his target rifle in his grasp and was turning on to his side, trying desperately to aim it. Leo raised his own rifle, swayed a little as he pulled it in tight to his shoulder, then shot Pike through the head.

The bullet had struck Merry just behind her left eye, knocking the mare sideways and dropping her to the ground. Nerys had instinctively tried to roll with the fall but she landed awkwardly and the breath was knocked out of her.

She came to rest lying on her side, looking towards the fallen horse and barely two feet from it. Blood pouring from the wound in Merry's head was on Nerys herself, on her face, her hands, her clothes. She had no idea that she had been fired at, the sound of the shots had merged with the shock sensation of the fall. She shivered continuously and her bloodstained face became ashen as clinical shock overtook her. She lay still with her head on the coarse grass, staring at the remains of Merry's head. Nothing in her quiet protected life had prepared her for the reality of extreme physical violence.

Eventually she lifted herself on her elbows and looked about her. It was a nightmare scene. Leo scrambling up the slope opposite, the man shooting him down, then being shot down in his turn. She watched with disbelief and fascinated horror as Leo Wyndsor committed murder before her straining eyes.

Then she heard her own voice, a thin high scream of terror and dismay. In a few moments her world had collapsed about her. Then Leo was staring at her. The distance between them seemed gigantic and they were strangers.

Far away she heard the sound of the approaching Landrover.

It began to rain, heavy pattering drops that splattered into the shattered side of Merry's head. Nausea overcame Nerys and she gave herself up to uncontrollable retching.

'It's all over, Miss,' a man's voice said from somewhere above her.

'I thought he had killed you,' Leo said slowly and carefully.

184

Nerys sat nervously upright in the hard plastic chair beside the hospital bed in the small antiseptic-smelling room. Her face was white and drawn. She had been crying. Sunlight poured through the shutters of the single window, painting broad yellow lines across the bedcovers, across her face, across her long auburn hair.

'I know,' she said.

Leo felt a kind of desperate lassitude. There was, he knew, nothing he could do or say that could change things. They were simply going through the motions that decency required. His cause was hopeless.

'Some women,' he said, 'would have been enormously flattered to think a man loved them so much that he was prepared to kill for them.'

'I dare say,' Nerys said quietly, 'that some women would be.'

She took his hand and pressed it emphatically.

'I simply cannot accept violence in any form, Leo. It sickens me . . . I can't cope with it, see?'

'Don't you understand that he would have killed me. He'd already tried once.'

Nerys stood up, placed her chair carefully in a corner and returned to stand by the bed.

'Exactly. You didn't kill for me. You did it because of anger and fear, for what he had done to you. It was murder, Leo, even though it may have been legal.'

She moved to the door. Leo could think of nothing to say.

'Goodbye,' she said, at the door.

He could not look at her. 'So, I have lost then,' he said finally.

'No, *we* have lost,' Nerys corrected.

And she was gone.

Some fifteen minutes later Bob Staunton slid furtively round the door, clutching a briefcase and offering a conspiratorial grin which Leo could not help but return. Closing the door behind him, Bob crossed the room and placed the briefcase on the bedside table. To Bob, Leo seemed to be taking his physical and emotional injuries equally well, but Bob knew that he must still employ tact.

'Just saw Nerys,' Bob said, opening the briefcase and taking out two small glasses. 'She reckons it's off. That right, son?'

He glanced sideways at his colleague, anxious to gauge Leo's reaction. Lovelorn assistants were a pain.

Leo shrugged. 'It was beautiful, but it was, well, only a lotus dream,' he said, attempting a nonchalance he did not feel.

Bob Staunton relaxed – Leo would recover. Bob grimaced sympathetically, producing a bottle of brandy from the depths of the briefcase and filling the glasses to the brim.

'Here,' he said, 'take your medicine.'